MAGICAL CREATURES OF MUMBAI'S UNDERBELLY

MAGICAL CREATURES OF MUMBAI'S UNDERBELLY

SNEH SAPRU

White Falcon Publishing

www.whitefalconpublishing.com

Magical Creatures of Mumbai's Underbelly
Sneh Sapru

www.whitefalconpublishing.com

ISBN - 978-93-89932-98-0

The strip of coastland, in the middle of which lies the island of Bombay, has been the gathering-ground of various races and civilizations, ever since the dim days when the first shipmaster launched his frail bark upon the waters of the ocean. The trade between Western India, Babylon and Egypt has been monopolized in turn by invaders from the north (Gujarat), the East (Deccan and Telingana) and the South (Carnatic), and has allured strangers from three continents to these shores. One after another, the famous ports of Supara, Bassein, Thana, Kalyan, Chaul and Janjira have risen, flourished and decayed; and swarm after swarm of immigrants from all parts of India and the world have mixed the population to an almost inconceivable extent and left to Ethnology and Anthropology a riddle which so far they have been powerless adequately to solve.

- Bombay City Gazeetteer, Volume ii

*To the tectonic plates that set the stage for
this city and its tales.*

*To Rahul and Gayatri, who trusted my craft
when I didn't.*

*To the readers, who entrust me
with their imagination.*

CONTENTS

1

KAMATHIPURA

10

EXISTENTIAL
KISSY

21

PRAYER OF
TEARS

36

EARTH OF
EMOTIONS

50

KONJU VERSUS
THE CITY

68

THE SURVEY
METER

78

HERO DE NOVO

94

KIDNAPPERS OF
KOLIWADA

109

THE LOST
GODDESS

1

KAMATHIPURA

Siddharth shouldn't have worn sticky polyester pants on a stuffy summer night. Sweat trickled down his dangling privates where it settled between uncomfortable folds of skin and body hair. Humidity hung thicker than the musty blankets used as makeshift partitions, in the many whorehouses that dotted lane number 13 in Kamathipura. The smell of dog piss mixed with sweat and cheap, bottled deodorants overwhelmed his wits. Betel-leaf chewing *chakkas*[1] hurled girls as young as thirteen at him with faces full of garish make-up, baby cheeks and sickly arms. The *dhinchak*[2] thump of Bollywood music, punctuated by the staccato croak of police vans, buzzed through his eardrums in disorienting soundwaves. He was out of place, being

---

1 eunuchs
2 something flashy, bling

where he was. It helped that he was drunk. He'd downed one more peg of Old Monk over the one that was decidedly his last in a bid to up his nerves. This was his big night - the night he'd decided to lose his virginity. He wasn't expecting a porn film to play out, although he'd imagined his face on every single *porntastic.com* video he watched during his weekly ejaculation ritual. He reminded himself that even if he lasted five minutes, it was honourable enough time. That if, for some reason, he didn't rise to the occasion, he could clear his tab and no one would know.

He wasn't as heroic as he'd have liked to be, nor was his penis- it was as aesthetic as a gnarly tree-stump that survived a forest fire. His balls were a different story - always clean, trimmed, toilet-paper dried; he hoped that would be enough to uphold his honour when the time to *do the do* would come. He walked towards the yellow door with eyes down, whores in colourful neon sarees grazed their braless boobies past his chest, expertly faulting those eventful corridors bursting with human traffic and sexual frustration at its seams. Their gazelle eyes belied the hunger of an apex predator. An ominous current charged the air. The streetlights outside flickered, electricity lines hissed from around the crumbling balcony on which Siddharth stood. A loud thud, a deep gasp, and a gregarious fall followed (presumably from the ecstatic bliss that was a signature of cumming into Medusa).

Siddharth's restlessness piqued. He'd heard many great things about the creature who lay on the other side of that door - the whore who went by the Instagram handle: @Medusa.

'They call her the monster show – the ultimate entertainer in sex fantasy. She appears in harems across the world every fortnight, without prior notice, and only for a short time. If the reviews online are anything to go by, then she's an expert at giving men sensations they've never had.'

His boss shoved the phone in his face, showing him the picture of a strikingly attractive girl Siddharth wouldn't ordinarily have dared to speak with. She had neither garish lipstick nor ghostly white power dabbed over her face. She was virginal, way out of his league.

'Are you sure she's not some kind of supermodel?' Siddharth stared at the luminescent photo in his palm uncertainly. 'Hardly looks like a beast of any kind.'

'Oh! I hear she's a lethal, little beast… Now, listen, you want your first time to be intense, unforgettable.' The boss was the kind of man Siddharth secretly hoped to become. Round biceps and white-washed teeth between which morsels of food were never to be found. 'You'll want it to feel dirty. It's part of the thrill.'

'I'm not sure. I mean, hookers are great, I suppose. But Kamathipura?' Siddharth smiled awkwardly, imagining her face when he came inside her; the thought of a red-light district dampened much of the hardening sensation in his pants.

'Oh, don't make that face, Sid. Kamathipura is the place of unspeakable history… The world's most beautiful women have flanked those corridors from Russia, Turkey, and England. Traders, soldiers, sunburnt sailors, and hardy men have turned to hapless lovers. Unread poetries and shattered hearts lie across those streets. Good men and women have turned to hellraising pimps. Children have learned the commerce of flesh. If you listen closely, between those crumbling shanties, you can hear whispers travelling through the centuries - the mourns of ecstasy, the howls of nightmares. Those alleyways are charged with memoirs of dark, forbidden desires. It's all there, somewhere between the decay. Walk into its last remaining brothels. Earn your rite of passage. Kill the beast in the forest, slay the dragon in its nest. If you want to be a man, Siddharth, do something that scares you. That's when you know you're no longer just a boy.' The boss man whispered uncomfortably close, the stench of the onion and chutney in his drunken breath reached Siddharth before his words.

'Consider it my treat.' The boss man smiled benevolently. A macho smack on the back, another rum and cola and tall-tales of tight cunts got Siddharth's twenty-year-old hormones in a tizzy. He was burning to *do the do,* ready to walk through the illicit gates of erotica.

The yellow door flung open, and Medusa's customer walked through a beaded curtain. He was a short, round, balding man who combed his hair with a cheap brown plastic comb on his way out of the corridor. His eyes were downcast, his knees wobbled, and his wrinkly-old face flushed a shade of orange. Although the man made no eye contact, the body language suggested something *intense, unforgettable* had transpired. Siddharth took a deep breath, straightened his shirt, pushed the beaded curtains, ready for what was to come. The smell of *agarbatti* was welcoming, though the room was uncomfortable—a matchbox-sized, lilac box with no windows. A small four-poster bed took up most of the free space, and an ill-fitted plastic side-table was adorned with a bouquet of plastic flowers, a quarter of rum and a pack of Gold Flake cigarettes. Dampness permeated the walls. A cheap china lamp flickered by the corner.

'Would you like me to change the sheets?' She appeared quietly by his shoulder, a sight far prettier than the pictures that brought him to her door. Her skin was olive with wavy, brown hair that fell to her hips. Her eyes were green as summertime grapes.

'I….umm..I…it's okay', he fumbled stupidly, wondering how a creature so fine had won the reputation of a beast. All his doubts disappeared. Everything blurred save for Medusa. She wore a simple peach petticoat and blouse, her taut nipples teased under.

'Do you like fantasy?' she played with her brown hair, innocently staring. 'Some men like to rub jam and butter first, others dress me as their bride, some want to dress like the bride and have me watch. Where do you want to start?'

She asked the question with startling innocence. His earlobes grew hot with thoughts of unspeakable desires he had spent so much time day-dreaming about. He stared at her feet instead of answering. Her nails were perfectly manicured; her toes were symmetrical on both sides. Everything about her seemed chiselled by the Gods. She was just as one of the comments on her Instagram page said: *a myth come to life.* She bent towards the table by the bedside and poured the Old Monk, sensing his insecurity.

'A drink always helps.'

No sooner did it reach his hands, than he downed the glass. She locked her eyes on him and came closer. She needed no intoxicants to get down to business.

'Your first time?' she whispered by his neck. His hair stood at the warmth in her breath. She smelt of spices and the salty sea. She pushed him down to the creaky, old bed, unhooking her first blouse button from which her rounded breasts teased. He imagined what they tasted like – the promise of nectar sweeter than peaches.

'Want to know what my first time was like?' she asked playfully.

'Tell me', the rising testosterone built his confidence, the Old Monk churned his insides like drunken butterflies.

'Telling isn't knowing, mister', she pinned him to the hard bed, her hands guiding his own up her cotton skirt.

'My name is Siddharth.' His throat was dry; his tongue was thirsting. He pressed his fingers against her silken, soft skin.

'Why bother with niceties when you've come for something else?' she paused for a second, holding his hands back from exploring the depths of her warm thighs. 'You didn't answer my question, do you want to know what my first time was like?'

Her honey-soaked voice turned hoarse. Her sensual green eyes flashed with a hint of something sinister, something muddy. The walls caged in with impending doom. There wasn't any time to dwell on such instinct; primal urges were at play.

She unbuckled his pants. He ripped through her petticoat. His hands caressed her breasts, slow at first, then with an urgent hunger. She pulled his face away from her ample bosom, her mouth closed into his lips, and she moved her tongue deep into his. He nibbled across her mouth and neck. She purred with growing intensity; he could hear his heart racing. Her hands grabbed his erect penis; he suckled on her nipples, feeling their tenderness between his teeth.

'Do you want to know?' Her tongue traced his earlobe, sending shivers down his spine. 'Do you want to know?'

'Everything', he tore apart the plastic packaging of his condom with urgency. 'I want to know everything.'

Her brown tresses fell over the curvature of her perfect body. She pinned him down as she got on top. He closed his eyes before the penetration, awaiting the pleasure that had no name.

She locked on to his hands with unnatural strength until he couldn't move out of her grip. Her pelvis thrust into him with unnatural force. His genitalia reversed, piercing his penis inward into his organs until it inverted into the walls of the vagina. The tissue of the soft, sensitive mouth between his legs was torn to bloody tatters with the vicious force of a hammer.

In a paranormal turn of events, a man drilled himself into Siddharth, throttling him by the neck. He pressed into his body with ungodly force.

At first, he froze with terror. Panic and pain quickly took over. Siddharth wrestled, buried under the brute force of the beast whose chest weighed more than all of Siddharth. He bit into the man's muscular shoulders; the teeth didn't leave a mark on the brute's waxy skin. The man slapped Siddharth's face with a vengeance, throttled his mouth before he could let out a scream. Siddharth's skin crawled at the touch of that grubby beard. The man slobbered across his chest, neck and ears. Siddharth smelled the sea in the filth of the man's sweat, sinking into the pores of his flesh. He felt dirty, violated, urinated upon.

With growing desperation, he opened and closed his eyes several times during the ordeal. The nightmare was relentless, real, and rabid. He was sure he would die before this was over. What kind of a monster would torture another human like so? *It's in your head. This isn't happening.* He was supposed to be at a brothel; inside a lavender room, with a prostitute he could override. But his body was telling him another story. His back was pushed onto exposed stone steps of a temple in a foreign place, his skin scathed with rashes while he was thrust up and down. He screamed for help. Celestial sculptures all around him bore silent witness to the desiccation of his soul. A demi-god tore his hymen apart.

'Stop, please stop'. The man bit into his lips until they were sore and smudged with blood. His veins pulsated in pain from all over; he shook in intermittent sweats. The man pulled at his hair, then flipped him to his back, and pressed his jaw to the floor. His head exploded with pain, guilt, shame, fear, loathing, disgust, hate, confusion; it would take lifetimes to dissect the emotions that came with the force of the man's ejaculations. Siddharth wished and hoped and prayed for his lungs to collapse, his heart to stop palpitating, and his chest to explode. He wanted to leave that ravaged body and never return.

And his prayer was answered.

Hot tears streamed down his eyes. The familiar sound of the ceiling fan called him back into the windowless room with lavender walls. His penis was safe inside a condom. His cum dripped inside it.

'Funny how some people call this fun', whispered a voice by his ear.

When he turned to look at her, his bones turned to ash with dread. Beside him, lay a creature more terrifying than the ordeal he'd just survived. Giant snakes hissed poisonous fangs through her tresses, her pear-shaped hips were dark brown, with skin that crackled with electric rage. He'd never forget those eyes. They were giant, hazel and volcanic with dark magic. His gut turned over with just a stare. He leaned over to the edge of the bed, vomiting out blackened stones, maggots, green slime, then some more stones, maggots and green slime.

A hand offered him a glass of Old Monk.

'A drink always helps.'

He turned around to find Medusa[3] curled behind him, perfectly nude, with hair cascading down her breasts. He backed off as her hands reached for his, his knees hit the four-poster bed that creaked with a loud grunt.

'That'll be a thousand rupees', said her honey-soaked voice.

With trembling hands, he put on his polyester pants, buttoned his shirt half-way, pulled all the money out of his wallet, and didn't wait for the change. He opened the yellow door, a grizzly businessman with a giant paunch looked at him inquisitively. Avoiding eye contact, Siddharth hurriedly limped out to the streets with a burning sensation in his private parts. Above him, the messy cords of electricity cables hissed away like venomous serpentines as the cry of another man rang behind Medusa's yellow door.

He weakly pulled out his arm and hailed a cab jittering at the touch of a pimp who tried to drag his hand into another one of Kamathipura's many doors.

***

---

3   **In Greek Mythology, Medusa was a beautiful maiden who turned into a hideous monster after she was raped by the Sea-God Poseidon.

2

EXISTENTIAL KISSY

It was an opulent Sunday sundowner on the fortieth storey penthouse. Sorbet clouds floated through the deck like perfect party props, eager to please the entourage of partygoers robed in spring-summer resort wear. Unrestricted views of grazing horses on the Mahalaxmi Racecourse and a sunset against the Arabian Sea gave many of the foreign guests in attendance a chance to echo the sentiment: *Mumbai's the most magical city in the world.* For the locals at the party, the ambience offered no respite to the sentiment: *This city has drained my soul.* To Kissy, the whole affair was an unbearable charade – the endless glasses of margaritas, the sickly spell of hangovers, the stumpy stilettos that balanced nothing in life. Gratitude and thanklessness were worthless pursuits and fashionable conversation starters at glitzy parties. Kissy yawned, eavesdropping on a discussion illuminating the advantages of real estate in Greece. *You know what the homes are like there?* A chirpy girl with a floral wreath in her hair quizzed her more sombrely dressed male counterpart. *Anything's better than here*, the sombre man adjusted his glasses self-consciously, staring into the eyes of the girl with dilated pupils. *They're like so much better; you'll wonder why you even bother being here at all. Like in two crores, you could get a mansion with everything, like everything! A clear, turquoise sea, a white Mediterranean home, pink bougainvillea peeping through every window, an infinity pool in the fucking backyard... It's like you're living inside a Pinterest board... Like what more do you want? It's unfair how much tax we pay for the bullshit life in the city.* The girl went on rambling. The man in the crisp suit with serious glasses grew increasingly smitten. Their conversation steered towards flirtier pastures. Kissy observed them from under the dessert counter wondering when the man would chance upon the tan lines on the girl's ring finger, probably from the wedding band left at home. She wondered what kind of an ape this sombre man in serious glasses would turn out to be: the type that could love a married woman, or the type who'd blackmail her after. As Kissy savoured her banoffee pie and placed bets on the nature of apes at the party, an excitable Moses crept up from behind her.

'Happy Birthday, Kissy.' He sentimentally licked her forehead, smelling of vanilla beans, much like his personality. Kissy liked him. He was a good flatmate: gentle, considerate, and didn't think highly of himself. It made her approve of him; most creatures were mediocre and didn't even know it.

'What's so happy about the day?' Kissy purred uninspired.

'I don't know', Moses pawed his black ears, confused. 'You were born this day... That's why the celebration.'

'Celebrating what? Another trip around the sun? Another round of degenerating cells? A celebration for whom? Gupps over there?' Kissy's vocal cords strained. Nothing killed a meaningful conversation like techno music. Inebriated guests burst into hideous laughter spells from jokes they couldn't hear. Somewhere between that garish mess was her pet Gurpreet - the ape-pet was obsessing over sauce bowls plated with the wrong *hors d'oeuvres.*[4]

'C'mon, Kissy. It's not as bad as you make it seem. Our ape-pets care for us. They're happy you were born. I'm happy you were born. That's why I'm here.'

Moses' simpleton view on life was endearing, albeit bourgeoisie. She craved for a more secluded hideout and prowled away from him. Crouching at the edge of the parapet, she settled by a shady spot behind the fancy barrel of beer Gurpreet had imported especially for this party. The theme was *Kisses for Kissy* (whatever that meant), and Kissy wanted nothing more than to be left the hell alone. Moses followed her behind, loyal as a shadow; his grey eyes earnest in concern.

'Why are you so cynical about everything?'

'We're cats, Moses. We're born cynical about everything.'

'No', Moses pressed on. The noisy bell hanging on his neck strap made him cow-like. He shook his head side-to-side. 'Your butt smells off. There's something that you're not telling me. Spit it, Kissy!'

Kissy relented at last. It wouldn't hurt for someone to know. After all, she wouldn't leave a suicide note when she was gone. The music grew louder, and her voice grew shrill. 'Look at everyone around you… Do you think they think about the things that haunt them? No. They're all running

---

4   appetisers

away, you see? They're running from *the why*. I'm the only one bothered by it.'

A drunk teenager flicked his ash over her exposed back. She snarled at him, flashing her sharp incisors. He stumbled away clumsily, spilling more drinks at the sight of her canines.

'Why all this? This big bang? This combustion? This carbon? This air? This water? This mystery? These atoms taking millions of years to make a web of landmasses and life forms, where probabilities and possibilities collide into mandalas of infinite consciousness, all left without the answer to why any of this grand mess is? Why these lives? Why these deaths? Why these falling teeth, greying hair, failing organs? Why all the blanks that we fill in between? Why should I suffer another day, breathe another minute, eat another banoffee pie, if I don't know the why to any of it? Must I be grateful to be some form or formlessness of life in this universe, destined to spend an eternity without answers? I mean, what's the guarantee that there is an answer? Or the answer, if found, will be satisfactory? What if the real purpose behind all this, is no more meaningful than the boredom of a Creator who craved for some company? What if the Creator decided to throw a party where any and every vicious idea can come to life and try its luck, so long as it's entertaining?'

Anxiety escaped her lungs in quick breaths. Moses' brown eyes were dumbfounded. She envied him because he would never know the burning itch of this unknowing.

'Why must I, the bearer of this *why* the rest of you so ingeniously look past, not find my own answer? If energy is infinite and I will go on in this universe with or without being in this body, then I've found a way to trick the Creator at his or her own game. I've hacked the system, Moses. I will kill myself at the earliest in each life and live on as a new life form in some other dimension. On and on, I will go until I find that sadistic Creator. And that is why Moses, tonight I will die.'

Moses' soft pink nose turned to the colour of a rash. 'Wait… But you're a cat. We have nine lives.'

From across their table, the thumping feet on the dance floor made way for a food tray. Gurpreet pushed a tuna cake for cat consumption, shaped in the number five, which she mistook to be Kissy's age despite the thirty-six cat years she had endured. There was also another, much larger, red-velvet cake for human consumption along with wafers, sandwiches and sodas, also meant for human consumption to celebrate Kissy's birthday. The DJ in the oversized T-shirt and cigarette pants pumped up the bass, blasting a cringe-worthy happy birthday song. Guests clapped on with ridiculously large smiles on their faces. Gurpreet announced aloud.

'Anyone seen Kissy? *My jaan*[5]? My little ball of grey?'

Kissy licked Moses' dumbstruck mouth hurriedly. Time to exit the matrix had come. 'You be good, dear Moses.'

Before Moses could spoil her plan, or Gurpreet would come down and swoop her up for the cake-cutting, Kissy blew the candles of her life. Hurriedly, she snuck to the corner of the table where stacked cardboard boxes made a perfect ladder to the parapet, past which there was nothing but her and the fall to death. *There she is, the birthday girl,* the girl with the floral wreath pointed to Kissy excitedly, while slurring mildly. Kissy turned her back to the crowd,

---

5   my love

and without looking down, for fear of changing plans, she made the leap of faith.

Like a movie scene playing in slow-motion – the error of judgement dawned upon her - she hadn't fallen forty storeys at all. She had jumped off the wrong corner, one where a neighbour on the thirty-third floor had extended his balcony (unlawfully), manicuring an indulgent terrace garden for his little children. Kissy remembered the taste of idiocy on her tongue - that acidic sting of bile, skidding onto a turquoise slide, flying a couple of feet in the air, before her head landed on an ornate ceramic pot, and she lost consciousness. Like a bullet separating from the gun, Kissy split into something else. Her physical body hit the ground. *Why does a cat have nine bloody lives?*

Weightless as a feather, she floated on her neighbour's terrace, watching squeaking children on the garden rush to their parents' bedroom. Weightless as a memory, she floated to the fortieth terrace where Gurpreet's mouth was open in horror, and Moses hung by the edge of the parapet, watching his friend's mangled body seven storeys below. Weightless as a whisper, she reached towards the stratosphere, and a cold chill passed through her being, minty as a boutique hotel's towel. Up, up and away she went until there was nothing but the blue sky; she was nothing but a translucent something. A giant cloud, shaped like a cat, floated towards her. The cat looked restful, wrapped in a monk's robe, serene like the Buddha.

'Hello there, Kissy', the Buddha Cat spoke without opening its mouth.

'I knew you were a cat', Kissy sniggered. 'Who else could be so sinister?'

'I am what you need me to be', the Buddha Cat smiled, eyes still closed. The cloud was so still, Kissy could well be conversing with a stone.

'I needed you to be good, fair and kind… You've strayed far from those things. First, you make the dinosaurs, then the cat kingdom ruled the world. Then, the apes hunted tigers and killed every other species. Now the apes are killing themselves and everything else.' Kissy's cheeks flushed angrily. She was furious at the chaos of creation. 'Don't even get me started on what you're doing with the rest of the animal kingdom. I mean, just thinking about the cats in Syria and Sudan makes me sick.'

The Buddha Cat listened with equanimity (although there was no way to know for sure since it didn't open its eyes).

'Wait a minute', Kissy raised her eyebrow, 'You're still playing games here, aren't you?'

'I'm always playing games, Kissy', the Buddha Cat said. 'And so are you.'

'So, this is a game?' She looked at the Creator without feeling a sense of smallness - a cloud thousand times bigger than her misty soul. 'What is the truth then? Is there any truth to this world at all? Or are you too busy having fun?'

'The truth is everywhere you seek it', the Buddha Cat's tone as distant as a recorded machine voice in an elevator.

Kissy's tail went up mistrusting. 'Don't you talk this stoner shit to me… I want you to open your eyes and tell me the truth to my face.'

'My eyes are open, Kissy. You're the one not looking', the Buddha Cat wasn't one for sentimentality.

'Oh, sure. Know it all!' Kissy spat anger at the cold cloud. 'Tell me where to look?'

'Down', the Buddha Cat said. Kitty stared at her manicured spirit paws, finding nothing different about them (except for the obvious weightlessness). Her eyes, like a shaft of sunlight, pierced through the veil of clouds, towards a penthouse, where a party had come to a stand-still. A crowd huddled over the shoulder of an ape-pet named Gurpreet. A black cat named Moses looked white as a ghost. Meanwhile, in a shadowy corner of that said terrace, a drunk girl's floral wreath fell off, locking lips with a sombre man grabbing at her butt while she tore off his coat. Lower still, an assistant veterinarian rushed with a stretcher picking the overfed, grey furball, Persian cat who'd turned to a shade of beetroot from the rupture on the head. Lower still, an elderly couple sat across each other playing games on their phones, over a quiet dinner. Down at the lobby, a sinewy watchman pinched a new-born baby in her stroller, while her daddy was out taking a cigarette break. Further down, worms living below the Earth devoured a plastic motif shaped like a leaf and choked to their deaths. And in the unexplored nucleus of the Earth, rock-shaped dwarves swam in a pool of lava, waiting for a chance to explode through the Earth's core and grow into burgeoning mountains as a sky full of tectonic plates danced above them.

'Left', instructed the emotionless, elevator voice. Kitty's sunlit vision field turned sideways where swirling particles of energy dazzled in bright colours of the rainbow, spiralling downward, through the clouds. Carried by the Earth's winds, they pollinated life everywhere - the bellies of expecting mothers and eggs in birds' nests. A blood-stained baby pushed between a woman's legs. Tadpoles took their first swim in muddied waters. Tiny buds learned how to fend off attacking birds. All around Mumbai, the rainbow light entered into the bodies of kittens, puppies, cubs, tadpoles, chicks, calves, piglets, joeys, pinkies, lambs, fish eggs, larvae, and infants.

'Right', came the directive of the elevator voice. Kissy turned her head and found spirits just like herself, standing parallel to her shoulders, facing their Creators on the conundrums of life. A brown horse saw his Creator coloured in his own image. *Who am I?* He neighed at the horse-shaped cloud, confounded by the dogma that claimed his earthly life. A businessman saw his Creator as the Goddess Laxmi. *Why did it have to be me?* He cried teary-eyed; hands folded in a humble prayer. An atheist saw his Creator as a black hole, staring wordlessly into its abyss before jumping right in. Kissy looked back at her own cloud, a Buddha Cat wrapped in a monk's robes with an elevator voice.

'What does it all mean?' she asked, overwhelmed by a universe much-too-large for her feline mind.

'Look up', the Buddha Cat said unfeelingly. Kitty raised her dazed eyes. A floodgate of new sensations rushed in. She soared faster than the speed of sound, heat, or her own paranoia, diving into a portal of neon galaxies where she was some odd sort of light. Her paws, claws, limbs, fur, everything was blurry as line drawings. She feared looking at her body parts, dissolving into smoke of variant colours in bright blues, yellows, and whites. She was no longer Kissy, although she was. And that kind of contradiction made her nauseous.

'Stop', she begged out loud to the stars, 'I don't want to see any more, I just want to go home.'

She missed her fluffy white bed, her cosy pink blankets, her tuna cans, and her vanilla friend Moses who she'd liked doing catnip with. She even missed Gurpreet, whose most severe personality complexes were so much simpler than the entirety of the cosmos Kissy had decided to take on.

'There is one place you still have to go to, Kissy', an echo floated between her left and right earlobes, buzzing like a fly. Every part of her was fluid, expanding, out of her command. Every quark was an anarchist. Every atom wanted its own free will. Kissy couldn't wrap her mind around any of it. She worried that her voice would dissipate just like everything else. 'I just want to go home.'

'The only way to go home… is to go through', the echo surrounded her, between the smoky, starry space. Her spirit no greater than a speck of cosmic dust. She was all alone, oddly overwhelmed by a companion who was nowhere to be seen.

'Oh God', Kissy's voice was leaving her, turning into a dreamy, fluid smoke. 'Where do I have to go?'

'Inside', the cosmic abyss smelled like a burning wick, the second it's blown out.

And then there was darkness. Not like black, vantablack or any other new blacker than black sort of darkness. It was empty. There was nothing there. Not a colour, nor a shape, a size, a dream, a voice, a whisper, the histories of a planet, an asteroid, or an electron. It was neither born nor dead. It neither hoped nor despaired. But it breathed. And because it breathed, it expanded. And because it expanded, it grew. And because it could grow, it had the freedom to grow in any which way. Energy expanded in every form, shape and direction of possibilities.

When Kissy finally opened her eyes, she was in her bedroom, with a cast over her left hind leg and a wrap over her head wound.

'You're awake', Moses sighed, choking with disbelief. 'This is pawsome! Absolutely pawsome!' he licked her face until her fur smelled of the chicken gravy he ate for lunch. 'I knew you'd return, I just knew it. Gurpreet knew it too. She thought you'd been depressed because she'd been working late. I wanted to tell her so badly the thing you told me when you jumped… I wanted to assure her that your madness was cent percent your own… But you know how ape-pets take everything personally… Never mind. Never mind. She'll be so happy to see you awake when she's back from work.'

Kissy was disoriented. Her dislocated hind legs were fastened in a cast. Her body spasmed in intermittent spells. Her head felt heavy and throbbed from the ruptured skin. The pink blanket she had returned to made everything better. Moses continued licking her front paws with fervent devotion; she felt grateful for his company.

'I've been praying, Kissy. I've been praying all along… I did not know whom to pray to because we're cats, and we don't do these things. Yet, the belief I've found is as comforting as tuna curry. Look, Kissy!' He pointed out of their room window where a fluffy cloud, faintly shaped like a cat, rested its head sideways with the Buddha's smile.

'It's been there since the night you jumped', the cloud reflected in Moses' giant eyes, shape-shifting into tinier soufflés that went off their own way. Kissy watched them part, feeling that ineffable gush of emotions she could never rein into the construct of a sentence, for as long as she was alive.

3

A PRAYER OF TEARS

Mumma was a good woman, an austere woman, a virtuous woman, a holy woman - by every yardstick of those self-appointed labels. She was up each morning, earlier than the sun, earlier than the 4 a.m. Churchgate local train. The first person to bathe, ring the prayer bell, boil the milk, prepare a sumptuous breakfast for her family: complete with fruit, bread, eggs, poha, chai, and biscuits. She had mastered the economics of martyrdom - of giving away food from her plate like that last *paratha,* stuffed bread, or her own bowl of *aam ras*[6] to impress upon her guests the virtuosity of their host. She prided herself in eating last and the least of all portions. She never failed to wear a *gajra*[7] in her hair and a warm smile on her face. Or massage her husband's

---

6   mango pulp
7   string of flowers

balding head and her beloved daughter's luscious, black mane with warm coconut oil every Sunday. She liked telling everyone how she'd only ever suffered from arthritis despite taking no sick days or Sundays off in the twenty-five years of her married life. Perhaps, the greatest of all her many feats was that the hundred-and-fifty members of her neighbourhood and even her husband revered her as *Mumma*. She was everybody's designated caregiver.

If a young couple fought in the middle of the night, Mumma swiftly appeared by their doorstep in her tie-dye nighty ready to play mediator. If an unruly parent whipped a leather belt across their juvenile son's arse, Mumma heroically threw herself between the buckle and the child. When a friend, relative or associate came to her door accusing her husband of fraud and forgery, Mumma quickly hung a rope to the fan, ready to choke to death than hear a word against her beloved Sarkaar. Mumma believed that God helps those who sacrifice themselves. Despite holding that esteemed connection to the powers that be, of late, all of Mumma's prayers to heavens were left unanswered.

'How's Sarkaar doing, *men*?'

'Same.'

She sat with her friend and confidant Pepsi, enjoying the afternoon sun. The courtyard was teeming with life. Children played an inventive game of cricket - using rolled balls of paper and their palms as bats. Old Shashi Kaka snored two doors away, sleeping on his paunch with his butt-crack facing the world. The Naresh family next-door enjoyed their loud and righteous *aarti*[8], praising their lord in unison (much to the ire of Mumma, who deemed their devotion a ruse).

---

8 prayer

'The doctors say there's no hope… Nobody knows what will happen', the *manglasutra*[9] moved restlessly between her fingers as she spoke. *Sarkaar,* she called him, her lord. She obeyed his every command.

'Have faith, dear.' Pepsi's grubby fingers reached for Mumma's support.

'Oh, I've had faith, Pepsi', Mumma choked back her disappointment in the Gods. 'Every day gets tougher. The money lenders haven't stopped coming home to spew their lies at my door. They don't want to leave Sarkaar alone. Not even in his sleep. Imagine if he hears them… My hardworking Sarkaar can't defend himself, so they're chattering all sorts of bullshit.. those filthy mouths.'

The ladies worked in silence, side-by-side, dissecting peas from their green fleshy jackets that fell gently into a metal plate. *Tak-tak-tak.* In Pepsi's company, Mumma found the validation she sought. It mattered that someone believed in her, trusted her family and its honour, that the legacy of the Kulkarni surname wasn't going to be a slow, rotting waste like her husband's paralysed limbs.

'Have you called baby? Asked her to help you out?' Everybody's son and daughter in the *chawl*[10] was baby. Depending on the context, the right one was expertly combed out of the three hundred odd-babies of the chawl. In Mumma's case, the reference point was easy - her daughter, her dearest, her Asha.

'She's busy with work. She can't take leave to come home.' Mumma's lip stiffened when she lied the small-white-lies, which made life a little less cruel.

---

9 wedding pendant
10 a large building divided into many separate tenements, offering cheap, basic accommodation to lower-income groups

'Uff… The market is tough, isn't it?' Pepsi fanned them both with an old magazine, glancing towards Mumma with the adulation that could befit a war hero. 'Heaven knows how you show so much courage, Mumma.'

Mumma's jaw tightened, her tone grew resolute. 'I have walked bare feet to the temple of Siddhivinayak. I have crawled through the Mahalaxmi temple till my knees bled. I have fasted without fruit, water, or words for months. I have chanted the Gayatri Mantra a thousand times. I have worn black to impress Lord Shani, yellow to impress Lord Vishnu. I have fed the snakes with cow's milk, served the cows with a daily meal. How long will the Gods ignore me, Pepsi? How long?'

Mumma's devotion moved Pepsi to tears. 'Sarkaar is lucky, men. I would never pray so much for that rascal, Joseph.' Across the courtyard, Pepsi's five children chuckled their way in and out the house door, playing hide-and-seek with one another. Her stiff shoulders bent closer towards Mumma's reed-thin frame. 'Sometimes, I dream of life without him. Sometimes, I think it will be better if he was gone… Forgive me, Jesus.'

Mumma's eyes widened at the brazen confession. 'It's those women, isn't it?'

'Men never change', Pepsi said grumpily.

Mumma peeled her peas in dignified silence when Pepsi spoke again.

'Have you been to Rudali yet?'

Mumma's face darkened at the name. 'I don't believe in such magic.'

Pepsi's rounded, kindly face crumpled from the pressure of displeasing her friend, 'The women of the chawl speak highly of her. And she only works with women. When Suvarna lost her cooking job, Rudali's tears helped her find a new one. Now she works only with the big television stars. She gets Sundays off. They gift her expensive dresses. And that old man Tatya Tau, remember his dirty mouth? His midnight rage? His wife put some tears in his tea. He's mute ever since. Haven't you noticed, his fits have stopped?'

Mumma couldn't deny Tatya Tau's new, improved and mute avatar. He lived only six doors down from hers - his croaky voice hadn't fallen on Mumma's sensitive ears for days. She eyed him, sitting across the courtyard with a newspaper held upside down. He seemed to be minding his own business instead of rattling off abuses at the children running past.

'Everybody insists that Rudali's tears work... Why not give it a try? Maybe, she could bring Sarkaar back?'

'I don't know if I can trust a woman who cries all the time', Mumma didn't approve of making a business of sorrow. Her deepest desires were best shared with idols - only rocks could be trusted to keep their mouths shut.

'Oh, she doesn't cry all the time.'

'Then what does she do?' Mumma asked inquisitively.

'They say it's more like some sort of therapy... a confession booth or something.'

'She must charge a lot.'

'Nothing', Pepsi said. 'She just takes a bottle of wine.'

That night, after Mumma made herself a pulao with rice and peas, she busied herself tending to Sarkaar's bedtime needs – his cotton shirt and pyjama were changed into a fresh pair. His limbs and torso were readjusted to avoid bedsores from the inactivity of his vegetating body. She stretched his muscles out, cupping his soles to motion them upward, downward and sideways, like the doctors had directed her. Next, came her least favourite part - emptying the catheter tray filled with Sarkaar's cloudy, yellow bladder secretions.

The watery poop in his stoma bag was as unpleasant an experience as sterilising his stomach tube. The room filled with the whiff of his excreta; it was a familiar smell, not a comforting one. The nightly care routine left Mumma with no appetite to eat the dinner she'd prepared. She combed her hair, brushed her teeth, and lay down on the small mattress below his bed, ready to recite her bedtime *Dhanvantri mantra*[11] until she fell asleep. For those who hadn't made friends with the inconvenience of life, sleep didn't come easy in the chawl. Next door, from the wall common to her house, the Azimi family's *kholi*[12] boomed with the awkward sound of love-making. The newly married son groaned lethargically as his wife's noisy glass bangles clinked up and down. Adjacent to that paper-thin-wall was another paper-thin-wall, where a single mother nursed her cranky twins who suckled on her breasts at the same time. Adjacent to that paper-thin-wall was another paper-thin-wall, where Dutta Bhau played a noisy game of poker with his belligerent friends, while his wife cursed angrily at the children, threatening them with severe consequences if they grew up to be like their father. Adjacent to that paper-thin-wall was another paper-thin-wall, where a young boy suffered from dysentery with farts loud enough to cut through Mumma's prayer and potent enough for everybody to know that he'd eaten too much of that stale fish curry which his mother had made on the weekend. No secret was safe in a housing complex with matchstick-sized homes and combustible dreams. Everybody knew what was on everybody else's mind, body and dinner plates. Mumma had never risked such exposure, but Mumma had little choice left.

———————————

11 the prayer of prosperity
12 room

The next morning, an inconspicuous woman wearing a white salwar kurta and a scarf draped overhead, walked towards the local wine shop. The shutters had just opened for business.

'One wine', Mumma used a more nasal voice.

'Which one?', the man called Datta Bhau, who lived a few doors away from Mumma yawned absent-mindedly.

'The cheapest.'

'Red or White?'

'The cheapest.'

With a bottle of red wine secured under her robes, Mumma walked to the next chawl. The red door on the third floor shook with hurried knocks. It creakily swung open to a shabby, stout girl with uncombed hair. She wore silken pyjamas and a preoccupied look.

'Yes?' the girl asked in English.

'I'm here to meet Rudali', Mumma said nervously in Marathi.

The girl's face stiffened. 'By appointment only. You can book on Facebook.'

'Please', Mumma pushed through the closing door with the bottle of wine. 'I'm desperate.'

'Only because I'm hungover', the girl snatched the bottle, letting Mumma into her kholi. The first thing Mumma noticed was this - the girl had the room all to herself. There were no extra beds, untidy piles of clothes, utensils typically stacked around every free inch of the walls. The next thing she noticed was the personal bathroom within the house, a rare and uncommon feat in the world of kholis. The final and most unnatural of all observations was a shelf dedicated to books. Nobody had bookshelves in her chawl. Nobody had space or time to accommodate them.

'It helps me cry, sometimes', the girl was observant of Mumma staring at the library with a look of confusion. 'I feel like Khaled Hosseini's books are my own autobiography.'

Mumma had no idea what the girl was on about. 'I'm here to meet with Rudali.'

'I am she.' The girl pulled out the cork from the wine, whisking two steel glasses and a small centre table from under her bed. They sat across each other on two giant and comfortable floor pillows. When she pulled back her curly hair into a bun, the young girl named Rudali grew intimidatingly business-like in tone.

'I turn a hundred and fifty two years old next month, and I don't enjoy the small talk anymore.' The words came out of her mouth with sincerity. The girl crossed her legs on the floor pillow, surprisingly dexterous for someone who claimed to be older than a century. She had strange tattoos all over her feet - arrows, bows and dots that may have been black in colour once but now looked like blue ink. Red wine poured into the glasses like it were a harmless cup of tea.

'A prayer of the tear must always be true. My ancestors have spent too many years crying crocodile tears to please others. You must respect their spirit or suffer their wrath. That is the only rule of this ceremony.'

She drank the glass with urgency, refilling herself with another.

'Drink.'

A cup was pushed to Mumma, leaving no choice in the matter. She took a meek sip. It was acidic, smelling of a foul, old fruit. The girl spoke in a monotone, the kind that sales agents use while reading clauses of an insurance manual. 'Now, tell me…Will it be sweet or salty? Sweet tears sprinkle blessings on loved ones. Salt burns the enemy's wounds. What kind of tears do you need?'

'Both'

'The spirits tell me you're a greedy bitch, aren't you?' the girl wore an impish smile.

'What do you want them for?'

Mumma tried not to take the insult to heart, 'With the sweet tears, I wish to cure my husband. With the salty tears, I wish to burn all those who call him a liar and a thief.'

'Wasting the tears on a man? Very well then.' Rudali downed her third glass of wine. Her lips were stained red; her tone was dry and stern. 'Be sure of what you're asking for.'

'I'm sure.'

'Final call.'

Mumma nodded, and something about the atmosphere changed. The air pressed against Mumma's skin as if it were desert salt. She felt drained like she was sitting under the sun in a hot, bare desert. Mumma dabbed a handkerchief. An unnerving sensation grew inside her. Her muscles tensed and tightened. The follicles of her skin and the hair on her wrist rose with static energy. A buzz grew in Mumma's ears - like a radio transistor shuffling through channels, like a distant widow's wail. Something simmered below the surface of things. It was hard for Mumma to understand exactly what it was. It was even harder to understand the intention of the question she'd been asked.

'Do you know what it feels like to live in abandonment?' Rudali's face broke into an unexpected smile, and deep crowfeet appeared by the corner of her eyes. 'Abandonment is a strange, unsettling, bitter feeling. And a wonderful feeling. You find a secret universe on your loneliest nights. Every drop of water in your body sways to the moon and its tides. Every atom of your skin remembers just which star it came from. And your heart. Ahh! Your heart pounds with the whispers of your ancestors who've been waiting for your quiet, listening ear. Listen closely.'

Her palms moved like feline paws, scratching her earlobes. Her doe-eyes welled with tears. Her gaze grew distant and pained. 'Can you hear their choir sing? Can you hear them say you're worthy?'

A vial emerged out of her pocket. She expertly secured the sniffle into it. After wiping her face with a tissue, she downed another glass of wine. Her hair swirled side-to-side, her neck moved in mechanical rotations. She thumped her chest, and Mumma heard bones crack from somewhere near the petite girl's ribcage.

'Do you know what it feels like to live in abandonment?' Rudali's perfect, rusk lips twisted viciously in an encore performance. 'It feels like drinking the venom of a thousand cobras, tasting the hair on a dying man's cock, sleeping on a bed of arrows. Abandonment is an endless, hungering pit inside your soul. It swallows every happy memory you ever had. Kills the last ounce of hope. And if life ever gives you a chance to be whole again, abandonment strikes with its feelings of worthlessness. Before you know it, you've become something else. A fearful, trembling creature that hates its own company. Now, what kind of God would invent a tiny tear to cope with such madness? What kind of...' Rudali choked on the last word, snot dripped out of her nose as she wailed, 'Gawdi..dish..'

A vial appeared from under her pyjamas. She fortified her fat, salty tears in it, wiping her cheeks dry with a fresh tissue. All traces of the emotionally charged performance wiped out of her young, flushed face.

'Alchemy,' Rudali shrugged her shoulders matter-of-factly, 'is knowing how to use duality to your advantage. That's all it is, really.'

The girl handed Mumma the vials of tears. There was something intimidating about her presence though Mumma doubted the authenticity. The air around them was stuffy and humid again, the static undercurrent left as untraceably as it had arrived. Mumma's quickened breath slowed down. The girl went on with her instructions. 'Pink is sugar, blue is salt. You can find the instructions of use on my Facebook videos. Don't forget to like the page.'

An abrupt knock at the door brought the ceremony to an end. Mumma hastily covered her head in a white *dupatta*[13]. The silhouette of Rudali's next appointment loomed by the door.

'Be there in a minute', the young girl wore a poker face. Besides her cheeks that flushed a healthy red, nobody could've guessed she'd just cried twice over. 'You need to go now, my next job is waiting.'

That afternoon, Mumma tightly latched the door of her kholi and sat down to find herself a moment of privacy. She followed the instructions Rudali had left on her online videos. She hadn't told Rudali what she really wanted. She couldn't get herself to take ownership of the devious desires scourging through her conflicted soul, lest it slip through the walls, and someone think badly of her. Intentions had a funny way of being misconstrued by words. Mumma's intentions were pragmatic. Most importantly, they were about fixing her family woes. Put into the world of words - what she really wanted, what she always wanted, was for the salt to erase her husband and for the sugar to bring back her daughter.

---

13 scarf

The following morning, Mumma awoke to the touch of magic. The tears had kept their promise. It started with a violent knock on the door, a usual start to Mumma's afternoons. Her husband's creditor Santoshji, towered outside their home, threatening to burn their room down if Sarkaar continued to 'sleep'.

'I don't care if he's sick, Mumma... I want my money back. I'll ransack this shack of yours, you hear me? I know the police, I know the MLA... I'll make your life a living hell.' Mumma raised her swollen eyes and pushed the curtains aside. Santoshji's gaze fell upon the only bed in the room. Perched on the pillow was Sarkaar, bluish-white as a loaf of musty bread. A corpse gasping for its last breath.

A helpless tear rolled out of Mumma's eyes when Santosh banged his fist on to his forehead, possessed with rage. 'That cockroach ate all our money... The scum is dead, that Kulkarni is dead.'

With that one announcement, many of Mumma's family woes were permanently put to rest. In her chawl, every family followed an unsaid rule - if a man passed of unforeseen circumstance, his sins and debts did not pass down on to his wife and children. They were burned or buried with him. With Sarkaar's demise, an era of great misfortune had come to an end. Sweet tears quickly followed suit when her daughter, Asha, returned on the *chautha*[14] of Sarkaar's death. She cradled her baby in her arms, tasting saccharine wetness on her cheeks.

'I thought you'd never return', she kissed Asha's forehead.

'I told you, didn't I?' Asha wrapped her mother into her strong shoulders. 'I'd come back the day that asshole was gone.'

---

14 a day of mourning and prayers for the dead, the fourth day after the funeral

'Don't speak this way about him', Mumma scolded. 'He was your father.'

'He was a liar, a thief, and a fool', Asha retorted. She was just as brazen as Mumma was not. 'He stole from his friends. He stole from me too, Mumma. He could die a thousand deaths, and no one would mourn him.'

'Ssshhh, now', Mumma wiped Asha's angry tears. 'Think of him well.'

In the months that followed, Mumma felt contentment which she tried to underplay for fear of losing it. Angry neighbours stopped coming to her door. She no longer had to make threats to hang herself by the ceiling fan just to prove her integrity. Her household expenses weren't burning at the altar of Sarkaar's medical bills, and her daughter showered her with more gifts and surprises than she'd received on her wedding day. A new mixer-grinder, a dish cable and dinner time spent enjoying television together were just some of the thoughtful additions Asha made to Mumma's routine.

'Sarkaar may have passed away, but you found paradise', Pepsi teased Mumma on her change of fortunes. They sat on the stools outside the corridor, dicing carrots. Mumma hastily turned to check on her neighbours hoping no one knew of the colourful, joyous insides below her widow's drapes.

'Don't say that', Mumma hissed. 'Not a day goes by when I don't think of my husband.' She was thrilled to drop the conversation there, spotting Asha make her way between a passageway full of scurrying children and flying frisbees.

'I'm starving', Asha dropped her work briefcase and hugged Mumma tightly. 'Tell me there's something good to eat.'

'There's something good to eat', Mumma greeted her darling with a doting smile, eager to serve the *Bombil fry* [15]

---

15 crispy fried Bombay Duck

she'd prepared for Asha as a treat after a long day's work. 'Would you like some tea as well?'

When she turned over her shoulder to enter the house, she was struck by an odd sensation. The air felt stuffy and dry again. A static buzz grew in her ears. Piercing wails and the shatter of broken bangles filled her eardrums. An acoustic pain took over, acute as manicured fingers scratching on a chalkboard. The plate full of freshly cut carrots dropped out of her hands and hit the floor like tiny orange disks. Pepsi stood up, alarmed.

'Sweet Jesus', she gasped with tearful eyes, moving a few staggering steps backward. From the courtyard across their balcony, Pepsi's young daughter screamed.

'Arrrrrrrrgh.'

Mumma stood paralysed, coping with that which her eyes saw, and her head couldn't rationalise. It started with Asha, travelling to Pepsi, Pepsi's daughter, Shashi Kaka, the Naresh family, Dutta Bhau, Suhasini, and Azimi family. Only the infant children and the pets of the chawl remained unscathed. They ran helter-skelter through the once busy passageways, screaming hysterically for missing parents whose bodies of flesh and blood morphed into formless black robes, swirling on an invisible axis. Out from the cocoon of those dark robes appeared the ghosts of old women. They floated towards Mumma in their *black odhnis*[16]. Mumma fell to her knees, staring aghast. The faces of the women were older than the hands of time, their necks were tattooed with sorcerous symbols; their grey and cataract eyes were unblinking.

'A prayer of the tear must always be true.' The old women hissed in unison, slow as rattlesnakes, slithering towards

---

16 the head scarf traditionally worn by the Rudali clan

Mumma's door. 'The salt has burned every person that called your husband a liar and a thief, and the sweet shall bring him back to life. The prayer of a tear can never lie.'

Mumma crawled back into her kholi, slammed the entry shut with shaking hands. The hiss of their wails crept through the windows, seeping through cracks in the walls where patchy paint flaked off the ceiling with growing reverberations. 'The salt has burned every person that called your husband a liar and a thief and the sweet shall bring him back to life. The prayer of a tear can never lie.'

Cornered against the door, Mumma tasted the salt in her own frightened tears. Salt that poured down her cheeks, chin, and neck; until every drop she cried left her throat dry as the desert winds, stinging with the potency of a thousand needles, leaving her breathless and choked. From the single bed on which her husband once lay, ashen white feet touched the ground. His moon-lit face rose from the pillows. He sat back up again. Sarkaar's thin, chapped lips parted. He took a deep breath back into the world of the living.

'They tell me you've been praying for me, Mumma. They tell me you wanted to bring me back to life. They tell me I'm a lucky man.' His lips twisted in a sadistic curl, 'Am I really such a lucky man?'

Mumma met his cavernous eyes with a voiceless scream.

** "Rudali" (roo-dah-lee), literally translated as a "weeping woman" is a traditional sub-sect in certain areas of India. Women of a lower caste are hired as professional mourners upon the death of upper-caste males.

4

THE EARTH OF EMOTIONS

Aslan sulked in the shadowy corner of the empty men's compartment. The air was stale, passing through the tightly knotted grills caked with betel-leaf stains, phlegm and gunk. Mugginess clung to his skin like ash; everything smelled of cyanide and unhappiness. In the to-and-fro between twenty station junctions of Churchgate to Kandivali, his school sweetheart had graduated to a new lover. His vacant hands mocked him. They'd been fastened securely into Ayesha's only a few hours ago. He loved the tenderness of her touch; every part of her was soft as cotton balls. She had none of the rigid heaviness that came with bones. Ayesha, of course, was more than a cuddle-buddy, teddy bear.

'We're adults now', she declared seriously. 'Do you know what it means to be an adult, Aslan?'

'We can drink at a bar? I mean, officially', he closed in for a lick of the ice-cream in her hand, hoping intimacy would diffuse the escalating tension between them. They sat side-by-side on Marine Drive at sunset; it was meant to be the golden hour of romance. 'Do you want to go now? Get drunk and do other stuff?'

'No', she huffed. 'We have to break up.'

Her face was expressionless, flat as cardboard, mouthing words that ripped through Aslan's flesh with the viciousness of a carnivore. He avoided looking into those large, brown eyes of hers. Instead, he focussed on the ice-cream at hand - the one thing they still shared between them. As he closed in for another lick, she flung the treat, it landed on tetrapods by the sea and melted as pathetically as Aslan's heart.

'I'm serious, Aslan. My parents want me to see a boy this week', she stared at him distantly. 'I don't want you to feel cheated when that happens. It's best we both move on before I see him… This relationship didn't have a real future, anyway.'

'You're joking, right?' his voice cracked, sounding more like an animal's grunt than a lovelorn boy's plea. His legs felt weak. The blood slowly drained off his brain cells. It was painfully cruel to be burdened by the weight of such puzzling emotions on such a busy, seaside promenade.

'Why will I joke? You always said I don't have a good sense of humour.' She shot him an accusing glance. He knew what that expression meant. It was a cue to lather her up with praise, tell her how special she was.

He swallowed his pride, croaking earnestly. 'I love you. I'll love you till my last breath… We'll die together…'

'With our corpses holding hands… So that the excavators of the future will find us in the dirt and see for themselves that love transcends time?' She finished his sentence, scoffing at the greatest declaration of loyalty ever made by a boy to a girl. Her lips twisted cruelly. 'I'm still not sure if that was weird or cute. Honestly, I'm not sure I'm into you anymore.'

'Are you on your period?'

She ignored him as she often did during arguments, certain that her point of view was most worthy of the world. Her voice strained. Her eyebrows met with tired aggression as she repeated herself. 'It's not like we have a future.'

'Why not?' His scream caught the attention of teenage girls sitting right beside them. They shot him an accusatory glance - their inner feminists on fire.

'You always do this', Ayesha wiped fat, blubbery tears on her frilly peach top. 'I always told you we could never be. And you never listened. Now… now you're acting crazy. Like we hadn't discussed this before?'

The young, quarrelling lovers amassed an audience of passing families, and vendors promoting all kinds of services, from neck massages to boot polishing. A romantic sunset rendezvous turned into an ugly soap opera for all to see.

'You always knew we were from different religions. You're Parsi, I'm Jain. You'll be eaten by vultures when you're dead. I'm vegetarian, so I don't want my husband to go out like that. It's completely gross. I mean, think about it? An inter-faith marriage? It's two different worlds. It's a lot of work, Aslan. Not a very adult decision. It's stupid. It's as stupid as your plan to hold hands and die together. That's not real life shit.'

She blabbered on, breathless, choking. For the life of him, Aslan couldn't fathom Ayesha's obsession with marriage or religion - she liked keeping fasts, eating food without potatoes or garlic, and wearing masks over her mouth on the days she felt guilty of *'killing too many germs'*. She also liked leather bags and didn't see any contradiction in wearing animal hide so long as she didn't eat it. In retrospect, Aslan should've objected. He looked at her flushed, pearl face, her quivering lips, her perfect brown eyes, and erupted with volcanic rage.

'You're a really stupid bitch!'

There was a lot to be said. Words gurgled somewhere soundlessly behind his Adam's apple. The crowd swelled up to about twenty people, gasping in disapproval. *'Halkat'*,[17] sniggered an angry girl from the side, throwing her waste peanut cone towards Aslan. It flicked past his face with the passing sea breeze and burned like a slap across his cheek. His heart was racing. His eyes felt moist. He was uneasy with the insult of it all. Hormones raged in a language he couldn't understand. All he knew for certain was rage. An anger so potent, it wouldn't stop until he'd hurt her right back. Only an app on his phone could gratify such instinct. He wondered what post to put, what song to pick, which girl to flirt with. He wasn't going to let Ayesha know she'd decimated his self-esteem so terribly. Instead, he was going to philander because he knew she'd be stalking him online like a hawk, at this very moment. *What if she isn't stalking me?* His stomach twisted in a cruel knot, wondering if she would snitch him out to their common friends, as angry exes customarily did. What would everyone think of him once they knew him in ways only Ayesha did. The narrative pastures of his noisy head grew increasingly gloomy and dark.

____

17 an overall mean and nasty person

He didn't notice the train speeding along the tracks until the rumble of a horn jolted him in his seat. Khar station passed by in a whizz. He'd gone from the heart of the island city to its suburbs in less than ten minutes. For a local chugging at less than fifty kilometres per hour, such velocity was as unprecedented as it was nauseating. Mouth agape, he arose from the bench, peeping through the mesh-like divider between his compartment and the next, wondering if any other passenger shared his surprise. Every compartment was empty as far as his eyes could see. On a railway line ferrying millions of commuters every day, it was ominous to be all alone. Dreadingly, he gripped his college bag to his chest, wobbling towards the exit door of the speeding train, ready to alight at the next stop. The wind gushed through the open doors, pushing him off balance. He grabbed a top bar and steadied himself. Aslan was inexperienced in the art of jumping off trains much as he was inexperienced in the art of coping with heartbreaks. There was no handbook in life for a teenager to learn the ropes about these things. No curriculum prepared boys for the inevitability of making tough decisions, or living with their mistakes. Jumping off that train could turn his flesh into a bloody mush. Aslan didn't have an appetite for messy things. The handrails clinked against each other, echoing angrily across the rooftops of all the deserted coaches.

'Hello?' he screamed helplessly across the empty seats on either side of him. 'Hello?'

The lights of another station whizzed past, so fast this time, he couldn't read the name board on the platform. His only hope of escape lay above his head. The lever of the emergency chain stirred excitedly inside its holder. Aslan couldn't tell if he was imagining things when the red chain, standard in every local he'd ever boarded, beamed with uncharacteristic iridescence. *To change train pull chain.* Something about that safety message felt misplaced. Surely, there was a typographical error in there. Aslan prayed the lever itself had no mistakes, even if its messaging did. Sliding to the corner of the bench, he raised his hand and pulled the metallic chain.

'You did it! Thought you'd miss the sign', a voice hissed behind his right ear. A steely face with a pointed nose protruded through the metallic divider between the backrest and the next compartment. A mouth moved fluidly between the metal as if the metal itself were liquid.

'C'mon, then', the voice called. 'Cross over already?'

Fearful of making eye contact with the steely thing coming out of his backrest, Aslan picked his phone, opened the front camera for an indirect stare. The steely face frowned.

'Is he really that thick?' A new grumpy, old voice from across the compartment divider complained. 'Good Galaxy! To be stuck with this idiot.'

A gruff echo reiterated. 'Idiot. Idiot. Idiot.'

A thick, muscular arm dented through the metal divider, reaching for his shirt collar. 'C'mon now. We're on a limited timeline!'

'Ha.. ho.. Wha...', Aslan's curly hair straightened from shock and fear. Surely, these were hallucinations of the most pressing and peculiar kind. 'Wha.. What if I can't come back? What if you kill me? What is really going on here? 'I..I..I.. I don't know who you are... This is all just in my head, anyway.'

'We're not just in your head. We *are* you, dumb-dumb', a saccharine voice sang. 'You can't fear yourself now, can you? We're all one, dumb-dumb. We're all one.'

Before Aslan could consider the answer, the beefy arm thrust through the divider and pulled his body across the metal partition and into a mundane compartment full of identically blue, steely seats, white lights, and noisy overhead fans. The only novelty in the compartment was his hallucinations.

A curious trio he'd never seen before stood across him - a grumpy, old, hunch-back male with a long beard shaped like transparent crystalline stones, a dwarf with three heads and one stump leg, and a saint in flowing, white drapes, with a rainbow-disc halo.

They all shared his curly hair and small, black eyes.

'Are you all ghosts? I have an aversion to them… You could say I'm allergic, not that I've ever met one… But, horror films make me sick for days. I hate gore,' Aslan admitted stupidly. The threesome were least impressed by his presence. The grumpy, old hunch-back grunted. The dwarf with three heads and one stump leg dug its nose. The saint in flowing robes with a rainbow-disc halo frowned like a disappointed father.

'Hello, dumb-dumb', the saccharine sing-song voice he trusted belonged to the fourth creature. A curious beauty with wings of a firefly and skin made of golden silk. Her hair was wavy as his own. Her smile warmed him like a cup of hot chocolate. 'I'm Savi, from the Small Earth.'

Aslan's cheeks flushed pink with a mild blush. He looked deep into her black eyes. Her beauty was magnetic as a peacock. It distracted him from the fear of spirits and spectres. He didn't rationalise how he was talking to a creature the size of his palm.

'I'm Aslan, by the way. Nice to meet you, Savi, from the Small Earth.' He offered her his finger, which she shook with the force of her entire tiny being.

'Oh, there he goes again', complained the grumpy, old man sitting across him. His beard made of transparent crystals turned a shade of turnip. 'My heart is racing. My endorphin levels are high. This boy from the Earth of Emotions is at it all the time.'

'What did I do to you?' Aslan snapped at the old, irritable fool.

'Oh, you poor little dumb-dumb. What we do to one, we do to all.' Savi eyed Aslan sympathetically, like one would an abandoned kitten who knew nothing about the ways of the world. Her charitable fingers petted his stubble. Aslan wondered who these curious companions in his empty train were.

The saint draped in flowing, white drapes with curly hair and a rainbow-disc halo was quick to explain. 'I'm sorry for pulling you through the metal divider, but we had to intervene. We know you're going through the ups and downs of your teenage years, and you have our sympathies. Yet, the intensity of your emotions is disrupting all our lives. You need to control them. Our universe hangs in a delicate balance of our actions. The thread of consciousness weaves itself into another, making the fabric of space-time. If one thread is loose, everything risks being frayed.'

The saint's rainbow-disc halo rotated. His chest appeared to be illuminated, bright as a china lamp. Aslan felt a distinct sense of familiarity.

'You? You're the voice in my head?'

There was no denying about that silvery tone. He'd heard it right before every nervous school exam, every time his parents fought, every time Ayesha said she'd dump him. The saint nodded with an acknowledging smile. His rainbow disc grew bigger as Aslan's finger pointed towards him.

43

With a deeply distrustful gaze, Aslan looked at the four of them, rationalising they were more than just hallucinations, or some sort of delirium. They were signs of a mental breakdown. Ayesha had often categorically emphasised the words: *You're imbalanced, Aslan.* Maybe, there was some truth in it. Maybe, that was the only true thing about him. A sadness washed over Aslan's being, like delicate flowers wilting in a flood. None but Ayesha knew him under his skin, and even she was repulsed by what she had found.

The fixtures, screws, fans, lights, handrails, and floorboards reverberated as violently as his quaking soul. The wind echoed the muffled cry he tried to hold back. He looked at the four strangers around him; their faces mirrored his panic.

'You're doing it again', the saint sighed. His rainbow-disc halo whirled with dizzying speed. 'You're rattling our worlds.'

'That's impossible', Aslan yelped, pulling away from them, running towards the end of the compartment. 'I don't even know you, weirdos!'

He cowered in the passageway between the last benches, bent on the dirty floor, praying the tormentors would disappear when he opened his eyes again. Everything around him felt alive, imploding. The friction of the wheels on the track amplified in his ears, the exhaustion of the engine felt as laboured as his own breath. *I'm fucked. I'm fucked. I'm fucked*, echoed three gruff voices inside his head. He hugged his shoulder bag closer to his chest. The surface of his palms and feet were sweaty. He'd lost the only girl who kept his head in order, and now he couldn't even escape his dark, unstable mind on an empty train.

There, there. Aslan from the Earth of Emotions. The truth is never a linear tale. You can open your eyes when you're ready. The saint with the rainbow-disc halo sat right beside him, every part of him illuminated like a china lamp. The grumpy, old man with a beard made of transparent stones, scratched his crystalline stubble. Sparkling dust poured into his palms like flakes of salt. He offered it to Aslan.

'Try this, Aslan from the Earth of Emotions.'

Aslan licked the crystals, feeling a crunch like chips in his mouth. A moment later, a feeling of great calm and equanimity spread through his overworked, frazzled synapses. Everything felt quiet. Orderly as it should be. Savi from the Small Earth sat on the curvature of his earlobes and stroked his hair.

'Maybe we should have introduced ourselves better', the saint with a rainbow disc over his head offered reflectively. 'I'm All from the Wise Earth.'

All from the Wise Earth pointed to the grumpy, old, hunch-back man with the transparent beard. The old man acknowledged Aslan with a stern nod. 'This is Baal from the Earth of Understanding. And this is...'.

He motioned his hand towards the quietest of the group - the three-headed dwarf, with one stump leg, who chimed collectively.

'SONAR from the Earth of Echoes. SONAR from the Earth of Echoes. SONAR from the Earth of Echoes.'

Their grubby voices struck a chord of fear in Aslan. His muscles stiffened, teeth clenched.

'You're the evil voice... You don't let me forget anything. Every thought plays in loops.'

'Loops. Loops. Loops', the three heads of the dwarf sang in unison.

'We're parts of the whole, Aslan... versions of the same consciousness experiencing itself as every possible probability. We're all each other's consequences, each from a parallel earth. When seen from the top, we appear to be singular. When looked at sideways, we are many. You see, everything that can be, is. And everything that is, can be infinitely more. It's all about the angles, perspectives, or what have you. Tricky fractals to play with. Once you figure it out, you'll notice it's the most obvious thing in the world. There're more of us out there, but we can't bring everybody in one train, there're just not enough compartments. Although, if you saw all of us - if you saw yourself as a collective of the brilliant, beautiful, and variant spirits we are, maybe you'd take better responsibility for your feelings. Maybe, you'd realise that Aslan from the Earth of Emotions balances every other Earth where his consciousness resides.'

'You mean... I'm never alone?' Aslan's chest expanded with a sense of significance. A rapturous sense of wonder took over him, like being humbled by the sight of a great mountain.

'Never', Savi from the Small Earth whispered sweetly by his ear.

'And you're not my soulmate?' he asked disappointedly.

'No. Not in the Earth of Emotions kind of way', she said with a small smile. 'I'm a part of you, and you're a part of me. Together, we travel the multiverse on our own distinct paths.'

Aslan was a stranger to the idea of a hive mind. His staple diet of thoughts could be compartmentalised into three broad categories—excited, anxious or depressed. Every idea had one centrepiece - *him*. To see himself as an observer was as novel an idea as an apple being able to paint itself in a still-life portrait. He was riveted by his own uniqueness, feeling gentle sensations across his toes and fingers. His inner eyelids flashed with the colour pink. Slowly, but surely, the wheels of the train slowed down. Everything from the windows, the handrails and Aslan's restless heartbeat came to a standstill.

'Thank you', Aslan sighed. His muscles relaxed. His gritted teeth unclenched.

Baal from the Earth of Understanding gave him another dose of the magic crystals from his beard.

'One for the road', the old, grumpy man guffawed.

All from Wise Earth extended his strong, helpful hand. Aslan stood back on his feet. He looked at the foursome with eyes and hair like his own and whispered with gratitude.

'Thank you so much… You've given me such a sense of wholeness. You're me and I'm you. Always together. Never alone. How wonderful!'

The saint with a rainbow-disc halo and chest shining bright as a china lamp had a knack for whispering comforting words. 'Remember Aslan from the Earth of Emotions, you balance infinite worlds with your feelings. They are potent, strong, and powerful tools. Use them well.'

'I will never forget you, and I will not let you down', Aslan replied with a quiet reserve he didn't think himself capable of.

The four new friends dropped him off the tracks, where the train had abruptly halted somewhere between Borivali and Kandivali stations. Aslan decided to walk back home and appreciate the quiet of the night, hoping to unravel the secrets of his glorious and multi-dimensional soul. The encounter in the train liberated him from the weight of being somebody. He had nothing to prove, nowhere to be, no one to become. He was glorious as an imperfect tree that didn't beat itself about being a tad bit crooked, or stumpy. Pausing at the wiry, old Peepal tree right outside the railway lines, Aslan wondered if, just like him, the tree had more twins. He wondered if the Siamese of every tree's leafy, green crown was buried somewhere deep within its roots - inverted branches mirroring the life it anchored into the sky. Perhaps, the tree and roots squabbled with one another each day about managing their chores and balancing collective resources. Perhaps, after a tough day's work, they liked gossiping about one another's shortcomings to the birds, ants, and mites which had their own twins to deal with. He marvelled at such rhapsody. It was empowering to brood on subjects other than his own life. He sucked a deep breath into his belly, feeling infinitely connected to the symphony of chaos. Revived with the faith that even if things didn't make sense in the moment, in the larger scheme of things, everything had a part to play. His expanding outlook came to a premature halt when a light flashed on his screen: *I'm sorry, baby.*

Three simple words and one racy photo sent Aslan's thoughts back into Ayesha's wonderous web of love.

On the train that remained stationed between two platforms, All, Baal, Savi and SONAR stared at Aslan's silhouette curiously. He was facing a tree with arms outstretched, smiling dumbly at his phone screen.

'I'm calm… At last,' Savi sighed relieved. 'We can all go back to our lives now.'

'Uh-oh', Baal from the Earth of Understanding scratched his beard restless. 'I'm feeling the itch. That growing, gnawing, blood-thirsty itch.'

'Heart. Heart. Heart', the three heads of SONAR from the Earth of Echoes confirmed Baal's growing doubt. They caught Aslan's wayward emotions, projecting and propelling it as their gruff voices sang. 'Heart. Heart. Heart.'

'He's excited again. His girlfriend just apologised.' All from the Wise Earth's rainbow-disc halo rotated in an erratic motion - from concentric circles to asymmetric shapes. The light inside his chest flickered, uneven as a heart rate. 'He's back to dreaming about dying with her… Holding hands until their last day… Obsessing over the happily ever afters.'

'If that doesn't work out, he'll break our spirit again,' Savi's delicate wings fluttered around restlessly.

'Soulmate. Soulmate. Soulmate,' SONAR jumped on his one stump leg.

'Maybe we should put him to eternal rest,' Baal suggested exasperated, scratching his crystal beard aggressively. 'SONAR can always be a voice in his head asking him to jump on the tracks, fall under a bus, consume rat poison… His death would hurt us all. But there'd be finality to that emotion.'

'Many Earths prefer an Earth without Emotions. The dimensions are a lot more stable. Destinies are easier to accomplish. Life is uncomplicated,' Savi added sweetly, fluttering by All's ears.

The three companions waited restlessly for the verdict of their leader, All from the Wise Earth.

'Fucking Earth of Emotions,' he cursed sentimentally, absorbing the flurries of adrenaline passing from Aslan's young soul on to his own. 'Why does it feel everything so much?'

5

KONJU VERSUS THE CITY

Inspector Kumar and Constable Shinde drove through the bustling lanes of Lokhandwala Shopping Market. The urgent wailing of the police siren dwindled against the backdrop of shrieking hawkers, squabbling shoppers, and beggars crooning nasal songs for a quick buck. Meanwhile, a flamboyance of flamingos enjoyed a fashionable runway moment between the traffic lights as the crowds broke into a photo frenzy, capturing the phenomenon for their social media feeds.

Inspector Kumar rolled his eyes in disbelief. 'What the fuck are pink peacocks doing at a shopping market?'

'They're not peacocks, sir. They're some sort of foreign items. Haven't you heard? Climate change is making them crazy! They were usually spotted at the Sewri Ferry. Now, who can say where they'll be seen.' Constable Shinde pushed his stubby neck out the window, surveying cars piled up on the road. The biggest bust of their career was only five hundred metres away. A spectacle of migratory birds was the least anticipated obstacle. Inspector Kumar and Constable Shinde were no strangers to the strangeness of the city. At their last major tip-off on Colaba Causeway, a group of college girls was busted at a fancy house party. One of them made an unsuccessful attempt of jumping off the police van, quickly losing all her heroic gusto when she sprained her ankle. At the women's cell of the station, the limping teenager narrated a ludicrous backstory.

'I know you don't believe me. But cocaine gets home delivered inside tampons all the time', the girl's pupils were still dilated from insomnia and amphetamines. 'Mother's swear! I'm not lying!'

In the far corner of the room, Inspector Kumar watched sweat trickle down the girl's brow. He would have preferred interrogating the girl himself, but gender biases were a murkier affair than cocaine cartels. His colleague, sub-inspector Sundari Mane had a reputation of being much tougher than her male counterparts. She stared at the teenager expressionlessly. The teenager flourished her tale with absurd details.

'If you leave money out the door, window or balcony… and call for Konju… Cocaine miraculously appears at the exact spot you leave the cash', the girl gulped. 'Anybody can do it.'

Sundari Mane smacked the girl hard across the cheek, where it left a burning red scar. 'You think this station is a circus? Do I look like a joker to you? Let me see you laughing when I call your parents to tell them that their daughter can miraculously conjure cocaine from the skies.'

Snot dripped off the girl's nose. Her lips quivered, she sobbed. 'Please don't tell my parents… I'll do anything you say. Please…'

The girl volunteered to prove her radical tale. Handcuffed, she walked out of the station with Sundari Mane, Inspector Kumar, and Constable Shinde. The eyeballs of every other prisoner, lawyer, activist, reporter, and do-good-nothing passer-by followed them. She dropped a bundle of five hundred notes totalling to six thousand rupees under the flowerpot of a wilting old, pink bougainvillea plant. Turning to the heavens, she screamed with desperation.

'Konju.' Pigeons lazing atop the thatched roof of the station flew frenzied.

'Konju.' The abyss was in no hurry to call back.

The teenager went into lock-up, waiting for her parents to bail her out. Meanwhile, a dangerous investigation against an international cocaine cartel turned into an urban legend for dope heads and college students. Inspector Kumar's taintless reputation turned into the face-and-butt-of-all jokes. Anytime he walked out of the Anti-Narcotics Cell, chuckles heckling *'Konju'* followed him around, loyal as a shadow. There was neither a face, nor a sketch, nor a record of a man named Konju. And as Sundari Mane curtly pointed out, it was presumptuous to assume Konju was a man at all. The case was transferred from Inspector Kumar to another decorated officer who pinned the escalating cocaine racket to a more credible lead - a Nigerian power couple named Simone and Deborah.

All that remained for Inspector Kumar and Constable Shinde were petty tasks - like fining marijuana smokers on Marine Drive.

It had been twenty months since they'd worked the case from the side-lines. And while their hairlines receded and wrinkle lines grew deep, every single small-time peddler, abuser, and addict validated the ludicrous tale of Konju. After months of investigations, the best tip-off they'd received of Konju's whereabouts awaited them on the other side of Lokhandwala Market. Their tipper listed the address of a dilapidated, one-storey bungalow. One with a wonderfully omissible quality to it. It lived under the shadow of high-rises, oblivious to the modern world. The bungalow had been abandoned for years. The porch was full of entangled weeds. Black wallpapers were cello-taped to every door frame and windowsill. It was the home of scandals and ghosts.

'This is the house where the Wadhwani brothers died', Constable Shinde whispered ominously in Inspector Kumar's ears as they pushed through the rusty gates. The Wadhwani brothers were an estranged business family. The elder brother famously shot himself. The younger one overdosed on untold substances the very same night. It was a high-profile hush-hush case, the kind that left a sprawling family home, without any caretakers.

'Careful', Inspector Kumar hissed. Constable Shinde nearly stepped on noisy shards of broken beer bottles. Faint whispers slithered through the living room. Constable Shinde tiptoed to the left, Inspector Kumar slipped out a pocket mirror, peeking through the slit below the base of the doorway. Through the dust on the floor, shadows moved and danced. He counted three silhouettes, but they fragmented into inexplicably smaller shadows.

'They're outside', came a hurried, deep-throated whisper. 'Get ready.'

The air was tense and stiff. Inspector Kumar's fingers curled around the revolver as he pushed through the entrance with gusto. A barrage of feisty birds came flying at him, ready to claw his eyes out. Alarmed by the cacophony of their rattles, coos, caws, and clicks, Constable Shinde hurriedly broke through the kitchen back door, screaming.

'Poooooollllice', his mouth swarmed with feathers, cobwebs, and dust. He hit the floor. His cheeks pressed against the dirt of the ground. There wasn't a sign of footsteps, not on the ground floor, or the mezzanine, or the dilapidated first floor above. Nothing out of the ordinary, save for cobwebs, peeled walls, bird nests and floorboards full of dust.

'I don't understand', Constable Shinde was aggrieved, his eyebrows arched in painful union. 'I heard a man's voice; there was somebody here! Where did they go? What do these damned birds have to do with it?'

With droopy shoulders, they walked back to their desks. Another lead had failed. Another chance to crack Konju's case went to waste. Later that evening, Inspector Kumar sank on his sofa at home, wallowing in self-pity, drowning his failures in a bottle of alcohol. On the dusty television cabinet lay a photo of him graduating as a topper of the Civil Services Exam. Right beside it was the photo of his estranged wife. He was a loser, even to his own reflection.

The doorbell rang. It was past midnight. Inspector Kumar had no friends, not since his wife left him anyway. His apartment was the cornermost on the ground floor of an old tower; even the building secretary sometimes forgot he lived there. It was improbable that a neighbour came asking for rations like sugar or milk. Curiously, he stared through the peephole. There was nothing there, except for a pistachio-coloured envelope. Inside its sleeve, were a host of digitally printed photographs. It contained a curious collection. The first, a photo of a semi-constructed ghetto with colourful homes and tin rooftops. The next, pigeons sunbathing on the dome of a mosque. The last photo captured a tiny sparrow drinking water from a mud bowl outside a pink-walled ghetto home, with the silhouette of a bearded man at the centre of the frame. It was impossible to say where these photos came from or what they were trying to say. They were similar to every back alley of Mumbai's most unglamorous locations. He walked back into his bedroom with the photos in hand, wondering what mysteries the skies withheld, what secrets the birds lay witness to. The room's lights were out even though he hadn't put them off. Someone was at his windowsill.

A voice spoke, sultry and deep. 'Crawlers love being fed on a platter, don't they?'

Inspector Kumar searched his pockets for a revolver, without any luck. He had probably left it by the door. The shadow by the window skid something.

'The revolver's here', she said. 'But we have no use for gun powder this evening. Conversations will do just fine.'

'What do you know about Konju?'

'Ah, crawler', she sighed mysteriously. 'You're a subordinate in this conversation. You don't get to ask the questions, isn't that obvious?'

'I'm no crawler.'

'Do you have wings?' The shadow had a tall neck and a long black beak. She was surprisingly cool-headed about breaking into a policeman's home.

'No.'

'Then, you are a crawler.'

'What kind of a bird can speak?'

'The kind that's blessed.'

'And where do you receive your blessings from?' He wondered if she was his weekly tipper, the one calling each Friday with a new lead to follow-up on. The deep-tone was uncanny. He'd imagined a voice like that belonged to the juicy, large lips of a mysterious woman, not a beak.

'For that, crawler', the neck of the bird sniggered, 'you must leave your nest and go to the place of the photos. Not everything can be served on a platter.'

Wings fluttered against his window. The room lights came back on immediately after. Inspector Kumar rushed to the sill. There was nothing there, save for a long, black feather, much larger than the one that belonged to traditional crows or ravens. That night, Inspector Kumar had trouble sleeping. When he finally caught a wink, he dreamed of crafty birds and their mysterious wings.

In his dreams, he stood in a briefing room full of important uniforms at the Police Commissioner's office. They looked at him with a reverence he'd known while topping the police exam. His voice boomed with authority. His chest thrust out. He presented the case of the mysterious feather without a shadow of doubt -

'Our investigations have led us to believe Konju is training birds to deliver the drugs… Which is why we haven't been able to find him on the streets. He operates from the sky. The most unsuspected means of transportation.'

The Police Commissioner's interest was piqued. He smiled at Inspector Kumar admirably. 'We'll be the first law enforcement in the history of the world to crack a nexus of birds. Use the resources of all our units. Take everything you need, Inspector Kumar. Find Konju. Only you can.'

On the cue of that compliment, the Unit Inspectors stood up dramatically, raising their hands in a salute to their boss. The nemesis, Inspector Godbhole, was insolent, even in the dream. His lips curled, he objected curtly.

'Before you transfer this case back to Inspector Kumar… I'd like to ask him, who's the source of this incredulous information?'

'I can't tell you that.'

'Why?'

'We keep our sources secret', Inspector Kumar said unflinchingly. On second thoughts, he decided to announce the glorious breakthrough. 'If you must know… She's a talking vulture.'

'A vulture?' Inspector Godbhole repeated gleefully. 'A talking vulture?'

The mood so full of adulation and promise instantly soured into condescendence and ridicule. The table erupted with thumping laughter – the Sub-Inspectors, Godbhole, the Unit Chief, the Commissioner rubbed their hands on the tummies, their belts bursting from mirth. Inspector Kumar stood between them, humiliated.

An ear-splitting morning alarm woke Inspector Kumar out of his shameful stupor. He'd slept a whole half-hour more than his usual 7a.m. wake-up call. A koyal chirped its song on the orange blossomed Tecoma shrub across his window. He stared at the bird pensively. It stared back, undaunted.

'Time is running out', the koyal chirped. 'Time is running out… Death will claim every crawler, and time is running out.'

Something strange hung off the koyal's neck, something that didn't organically belong to its frame - something like an amulet. He rushed to his phone and dialled Shinde, ready to track the mysterious cartel of birds.

'This can only be the work of Khan Baba of Mumbra,' Constable Shinde held the photos from the pistachio envelope in his hand, staring at the silhouette of the bearded man. 'Can't you tell?'

'Who's Khan Baba?'

'You don't know Khan Baba?' Constable Shinde's eyes were accusatory, as if Inspector Kumar had failed to identify a silhouette of God himself. 'His amulets bring people back from the grave centuries after their death. He can train ants to dig for gold. He once brought a rain cloud to flush a murderer out of his house. He combed a Djinn out of a widow's hair. I'm sure these birds have something to do with him.'

'Great! Just what this investigation needs.' Inspector Kumar's heart sank deeper into the troubled waters of black magic, talking birds, and a cartel with wings. 'Let's keep a search warrant ready before we get there.'

'We can't search him, sir. Not unless he wants us to!' Shinde's forehead had broken into a sweat from the heat of the moment, and of summer. 'Didn't you hear a word I said?'

After what felt like several hours of driving over unsteady potholes, they'd made their way into Mumbra. Over-populous, semi-finished brick homes dotted a dusty, uneven road. Behind the chawl lay the Darul Falah mosque, whose white dome and minaret were identical to the photographs in the envelope. All around them were a murder of crows and a kit of pigeons. Inspector Kumar sensed hostility and surveillance in the air. He followed Shinde towards a small pink-walled shanty. A gathering of fifty people stood outside an unassuming, tiny, black door. The visitors carried devout offerings - a catholic nun held a loaf of bread, a burqa-clad girl stood with a tiffin of home food, a Sikh businessman brought along a gift wrapped in a shiny, silver wrapping paper. Inspector Kumar and Constable Shinde were the only ones who came empty-handed. They were received with cold stares. Policemen were unwelcome in ghettos. In these parts, men in khadi uniform did not solve problems; they were the problem. Devotees cornered them like sharks encircling their prey. The twosome stood detained until the front door of the small hut opened. A petite, burqa-clad woman called in a thin, nasal voice.

'Men in khaki… Baba wants to see you first.'

They sat in a bare room with a wall clock that didn't work, a calendar from 1975, and a small cot by a windowsill on which a frail, old man, named Khan Baba sat upright. His white beard took more space than any other part of his body. His skin was pale and grey. The veins on his hands were tired and ancient as rivers.

'There was a time when birds were as much a part of a man's world as myths… Some brought the nectar of Gods down to the mortal realms. Others had powers to feed off moonbeams for all eternity. Certain birds, like the doves, marked the soul of departed loved ones. Swans were the carrier of wisdom. You see, when we lost their stories, birds lost their voice.'

Inspector Kumar hadn't come so far to hear folktales. He cut to the chase. 'Who is Konju? Where can I find him?'

'Konju', Khan Baba's tone went from cold to bitter, his frail head bobbed. 'Konju was like my son. I thought I saw his soul. It was my arrogance that made me believe I could help him. He was my greatest mistake… I should never have given him the gift.'

'What gift did you give him? Some sort of amulet?'

'I gave him something far more dangerous. I gave him the gift that sets man apart from every other creature. The gift that let him share his dreams and nightmares with the world. The gift that allows him to bring his ideas to life… I gave Konju the gift of the gab.'

When Khan Baba peered into Kumar and Shinde's eyes, they felt an electric current pass through their spines. Baba grabbed Inspector Kumar's wrist with surprising strength.

'Wear this amulet', his eyes were glazed as if he was staring into a realm past the chipped walls of his home. 'When you meet Konju, wear this amulet.'

He gave Kumar instructions, without giving him any amulet to wear. Constable Shinde sat hypnotised by the old man's strangeness.

'When you meet Konju, he will cast the spell of words, vex you into his words. The amulet will protect you. Don't let it leave your sight.'

'Give me the amulet then', Kumar offered his hand, ready to receive whatever Khan Baba had to offer. The mystic's gaze wandered off. He stared into the wall clock that didn't work. 'The encounter is coming closer. Go now. Go!'

Inspector Kumar and Constable Shinde were awfully quiet, driving towards the highway back to Mumbai city. Once out of Mumbra, Kumar noticed an amulet with a black thread erupt out of his skin at the exact place where Khan Baba had touched his wrist. Constable Shinde looked at him starry-eyed.

'Baba can do anything.'

'Oh! Enough of that!'

As their van moved closer back to the office, the APCO 25 radio caught some frenzied activity. *'Calling for backup at second pasta lane, Colaba, over'*, screamed a voice in

Marathi. *'White car breaking signal at Trident Marine Drive over.'* A voice bellowed on another frequency. *'Officer Awchat is down. Officer Awchat is down.'*

'It's a shoot-out… And encounter just like Baba said!' Constable Shinde stated the obvious with a mix of excitement and fear. 'They caught Konju!'

'No', Inspector Kumar scratched his head, piecing scattered clues into a mosaic. 'They think Simone and Deborah are Konju… But Konju isn't a crawler.'

'A crawler? What's a crawler?' Constable Shinde grew increasingly jittery. The pandemonium on the radio reached a crescendo. 'What do we do, sir?'

'We find the real Konju. We bring him to justice', Inspector Kumar dramatically spun the car around for a quick detour. 'But first, we need supplies.'

The car raced towards the south of Mumbai.

Colaba, by night, painted a hauntingly different portrait to the tourist-friendly one it was by day. Its dingy, grubby, dark alleyways were filled with gangsters, prostitutes, and drug cartels from around the world. Curious creatures of the night ruled those streets, conducting their business in the shadows. If forced out of the shadows, or cornered into a tough spot, Colaba's illustrious list of crooks didn't shy away from making some noise. Noises loud as firecrackers burst through the streets as police vans chased a white car with a Nigerian cocaine king called Simone. Meanwhile, his partner Deborah guarded their fortress, alongside her army of men and women from Nigeria, Brazil, and India, each of whom was out on adjacent balconies, aiming their guns at the approaching police vans. Pellets echoed into the night. The cartel pushed back the encroaching law enforcement team with relentless rounds of ammunition. They fiercely guarded the top two floors, where giant rocks of cocaine were meant to be intercepted.

But the real action wasn't set in the human world at all. Unnoticed by the eyes of the law, Cooroocoo, a white pigeon with a black amulet around its neck, conspicuously fluttered away from the crime scene. After a hard day's work, he was ready to reach his nest for a good night's sleep. He soared upward, towards safer ground, when a special sort of terrace caught his fancy.

A feast was out for the taking. And a flock of birds pecked on the grains. There were corn and wheat, apples and worms. A buffet spread unlike any he'd seen. The kind his cartel was taught to be wary of. *'Don't be feral with your instincts. If it looks too good to be true... it most probably is.'* Konju had listed endless rules for the gang members of his cartel. This one time, Cooroocoo decided to defy the boss's orders. He descended on to the terrace, pecking a crunchy grain of corn while greedily competing against the grey pigeon beside him. Unfortunately for Cooroocoo, that delightful pulp in his beak would be his last. When he opened his eyes again, he was inside an old, iron cage, smelling of dysentery from a fowl he did not know. The scent made him anxious. What really set his heart racing were the faces of the two crawlers with giant brown eyes, staring menacingly at him.

'Where is Konju?' the taller one with a moustache asked. Cooroocoo innocently coo-cooed like a pigeon, as Konju had taught him to do. The smaller, podgier kidnapper was a lot less patient. He held Cooroocoo's cage unsteadily in his hand and bellowed into his face.

'Speak before I tear your wings with my bare hands!'

As the earth and skies rattled inside the iron cage, Cooroocoo ratted his boss out. 'He's at the kingdom. He's always at the kingdom.'

Back in the human world, news agency vans sped across the opposite side of the road. Inspector Kumar and Constable Shinde made their way back towards the Wadhwani Bungalow in Andheri, armed with intelligence that no man in the human world had found. The white pigeon in the seat behind them smelled of stale cheese; even the air freshener couldn't conceal its stench.

'It makes no sense, sir', Constable Shinde's eyebrows arched as he tried to solve the final pieces of this jigsaw. 'We checked that bungalow. There was no kingdom there. I mean, kingdoms are big, shiny, grand things. We couldn't miss something like that.'

He turned around and pointed his gun to the pigeon, who had identified himself as Cooroocoo. 'You're lying, aren't you? You piece of shit.'

'Calm down', Inspector Kumar scolded. 'He's our only link to the cartel... Stop thinking like a crawler when you think about the kingdom. We're dealing with birds.'

Inspector Kumar's mind grew increasingly calm and streamlined. He'd captured a talking bird from the mafia, all that remained of his mission was to catch the kingpin, Konju. They entered the abandoned compound of the Wadhwani home armed with bird feed, a net, a torch, guns and their phones. Constable Shinde documented the incredulous break-in on his phone, every step along the way.

Inspector Kumar made his way up the empty living space, towards the staircase leading to the first floor. He tore through the cobwebs which were thick as curtains, towards a passageway that smelled stale as an old box of Chinese takeaway. The torchlight at night brought to fore the blind spots of the daytime — across the ceiling, between the peeled paint and dust, were a million tiny crevices.

'This is it', Kumar smiled impishly, turning to face the camera behind him. 'This is the kingdom.'

The red, pink and brown mouths of at least a hundred hungering chicks chirped aloud. They stared into the alien torchlight with a mix of curiosity and caution.

'He's a sparrow', Kumar let out a laugh, running a hand through his thinning hair as he caught sight of the chicks. 'He's a fucking sparrow!'

'Konju.'

The babies in their nest jittered, crying louder for their parents to fly back.

'Konju.'

A small sparrow sat on the windowsill at the end of the passage, luminescent under the streetlamp outside. His voice was icy. 'Does Khan Baba think of me well? Intuition tells me, not. Nonetheless, I do send him my regards.'

The tea-cup sized bird flew towards Inspector Kumar. He loaded up his gun. It was a tricky shot, a dart in the darkness. An aim meant to injure the bird without killing it. He aimed his weapon. As his sight steadied on the target, a cloud of bats descended from the shadows. They swooped with military precision towards Kumar. Konju was quick to exploit the moment. His small, sharp beak cut the amulet off Kumar's wrist, nipping hard. The gun fell from his hand, skidding further away from him as the bats steered its course. Shinde was chased down, tumbling towards the ground floor, flocked by a blanket of birds flapping around him, fluid and fierce as a tornado.

Kumar stood his ground as Shinde was swept away. He still had his net and a chance to catch the drug lord, with or without the magical amulet.

'It's over, Konju. We have Cooroocoo with us. We captured him…'

'Right outside Simone and Deborah's nest?' Konju teased, reaching Kumar's nose to meet him at eye level. 'For as long as there are wings in this city, I will have eyes… Did you expect me to be so organised if I were that slow? Lords from Cuba to Miami trust Konju with their trade without ever meeting him. You know what that kind of faith takes?'

Konju orbited around Kumar's head; his eyeballs moving in dizzying circles. He noticed a small black amulet around the bird's neck.

'It takes the fear of homelessness. The hunger to outlast an unjust world. The madness to overcome extinction. That's how Konju builds his faith.'

Kumar lunged at him. Konju would be no harder to zap than a fly, but he was a lot more cunning. The bird could only be caught by surprise. 'You're clever for a bird, Konju. Still, I've found your little kingdom. And I will crush every single one of your chicks before this is over.'

'Careful Kumar', a thin smile appeared on Konju's cunning, birdy face. 'I've been studying you for months, and I'm thorough with my studies. You know what I loved about your language?'

Konju had a flair for rhetoric. 'I love its adaptability. You can read, write, draw, dream, all of it, in one language. We bird folk had multiple languages. None of which were friendly with one another. They weren't fluid. Places did not want to be shaped by the language of alphabets. Alphabets felt burdened by the language of dreams. Dreams didn't want to be documented. And history! Oh, our history didn't trust the simplicity of chirps and clicks. We remained forever bound within those borders even though we had wings. And you… You could create wings and endless flights of fantasy even though you are a crawler.'

Kumar grabbed the net from his bag. Konju fluttered back and forth towards Kumar, warming up like a wrestler before a punch. 'The most glorious part of your language undoubtedly are your books. When I first read them, dear me… I read of a world before this world, and a world before that world. And those ideas birthed the kingdom.'

Kumar lurched towards the bird with both hands. Konju dipped, unperturbed. 'You want to know what the kingdom is? The kingdom is a dream. The kingdom is restoration. It is the resurrection of the real world. The true world. The earth world. A chance for us birds to soar freely again. Building homes between woods, not between walls. Tasting water from the river, nibbling on grains puckered off fields, treating ourselves to juicy berries. This is the real law. The true law. The law worth fighting for. And the only law worth killing for.'

Inspector Kumar struggled with catching a dot-like Konju. The bird's flight path expertly manipulated Kumar's eye movement like a pendulum. It caused a growing headache. Kumar grew increasingly discomforted and fuzzy. He chortled at the bird. 'A kingdom is every tyrant's excuse for a kill. You're just a power-hungry piece of shit.'

'You know what your problem is, Kumar?' Konju snapped. 'You underestimate every intelligence, save for your own.'

Inspector Kumar charged towards Konju with his net. Konju flicked his wings, swift as an opera conductor. A swivelling cloud of angry bats screeched once more, dragging

Kumar into a flurry of their darkness. He was pushed to the edge of the window. His body came crashing down with tremendous force. Though the fall was only a few feet off the first floor, Inspector Kumar collapsed over the frame of the window's woodwork. Screws, nuts, and shards of glass pierced through his backbone and chest.

When they found his body the following morning, Inspector Kumar's eyes had been eaten out of their sockets by birds of prey, until nothing but two crevices of skin tissue remained. Constable Shinde was alive between the reeds in the garden, but he suffered from acute shock that left him dazed, mute, and trembling. Five-kilograms of cocaine were found inside his khaki, and the Police force had to explain what a dead pigeon was doing inside one of their vans.

The Police Commissioner towered over his colleague's body, staring pitilessly into his ghostly face. He declared Inspector Kumar a co-conspirator of the Simone and Deborah's cocaine-nexus, citing the obvious evidence on site. The press and media outlets created a fuss around their new law enforcement superstar. And a tiny sparrow fluttered inconspicuously above the media spectacle, manning the gates of his flourishing kingdom.

6

THE SURVEY METER

Afra's phone beeped 11:11 pm. Her eyes chanced the number for a second time that day. A colleague from the cubicle across was most pleased, insisting that recurring numbers and patterns were good omens - a signal angels used to mark their presence in earthly life. It was a time of synchronicities - of events in life playing out in divine timing. Afra considered the argument. Perhaps much like her, angels worked the grind, kept God bosses in good books and planned life around heavenly appraisals. Angels marketed their brand of blessings to the tortured few who had nothing going for them. And after a whole week of working at a soul-sucking job, angels hit the forbidden bottle of wine and partied with devils down the street. Afra had so much in common with angels - they both knew how to make compromises and get on with life without complaints.

The green post-it hanging on her computer was an irate reminder of the unfinished task at hand. It read: *Madhuri versus Madonna* in her scrawny handwriting. A click-bait piece that likened Bollywood's evergreen dancing girl Madhuri Dixit's moves to Pop Icon Madonna's. The bottom left corner of the e-portal she worked for needed its bite of entertainment. Afra's job was to find the words, pictures, and videos to fill its hungry readership. It took an hour and twenty minutes to write each piece of fluff stuff. Afra submitted five such miraculous pieces each day. If her journalism degree was going to waste, its onus lay on the readership. Afra was a mere agent of the miracle, an angel granting the internet's wish to be entertained.

Her phone beeped with a notification - the rickshaw driver had arrived at her location. She swiped herself out of the office, ready to carry the work to bed. She looked forward to closing her eyes away from the screen, resting her head on some cushy, glossy rickshaw side-panel. It wasn't the best quality shut-eye hour on her ride back from Andheri to Thane, but it was better than staying awake through the ride. Midnight traffic jams at the Bisleri factory crossroad released an unprocessed rage inside her. The sort she'd sought therapy for, without finding solutions. Cramped between cars, trucks, and ninja delivery bikers zipping without a helmet, she was consumed by a quiet ennui – that there was no hope for an insomniac city. That if something was not done for purposes of profit, it wasn't worth doing. They were all fated for ruin, and they deserved it. Each time she waited at the signal for the lights to go from red to green, she dreamed of the entire city blowing up, or washing away. Of mangled bodies flowing in a tide of dirt, sweat, slime and plastic. Of people torn to shreds by atomic bombs that crushed civilization down to the bone in a synchronised Mexican wave. Doomsday was her idea of daydreams.

Just at the thought of it, she almost split her skull on the meter. The rickshaw she was riding in screeched to a halt.

'*Aye! Aaramat chalav naa*'. Ride carefully, she scolded.

'*Zaa naa lavdya!*' the rider said cheerfully. Fuck off, dickhead.

'*Kai bol la tu? Thamb tula dakhavte.*' What did you just say? Let me set you right. She caught the rider's eyes in the rear view. They were large, egg-shaped, glinting yellow from some potent mix of intoxication - sniffing whiteners, beedis, pollution or all three.

'I'm sorry', his English was smooth, his voice husky, his accent foreign. 'It's just been a long time since I spoke Marathi or rode a rickshaw. It's confusing sometimes. I expected Earth to be upgraded to tablet transportation by now… It never fails to surprise.'

'A tablet transportation? What are you on about?' His tone did not slur though his excuse certainly felt like a drunkard's. The rickshaw picked up smoothly; they exited the corporate compound, making their way towards the Western Express Highway. Afra kept him vigil by engaging in conversation.

'There's a tablet I can take that'll simply transport me to wherever I want to go?' Shadows of the night consumed most of her curious rider's face and body. It was hard to see anything other than his khaki uniform. In the headlight from a truck across the street, his curly hair flashed in a neon shade of blue.

'What is this tablet made from?' she prodded.

'Ether', he answered like it was the most obvious thing in the world, like he had to keep repeating this stuff and no one remembered. 'Our thought beams gave inventions to your thinkers, philosophers, scientists, even your religious leaders, but your insecurities always get in the way. This may be the last time we'll come for you.'

'You talk like you're not a human.'

'I'm not', he said proudly. 'I'm a Shivenittikukas.'

It sounded like shawarma or some variant of it.

'What is that?' she was cautious not to repeat his name. 'A race of people?'

'No', he said. 'It's a race of soul.'

Afra fished out the phone from her bag. She could surprise her editor with a freak piece tomorrow; there was no telling what went viral these days. A catchy name always assured click-bait. She imagined this one would be called: *E. T Autowallah: Superhero In The City.* It would pique the interest of conspiracy theorists and UFO hunters, both of which were groups with cultish inclinations. A much-welcome quality for any readership portal. She stirred on the rexine seat; it squeaked like a rat as she came up closer behind him. He gave out a peculiar scent, some sort of melting battery or a cat's burning tail.

'How many races are there?' she asked curiously.

'More than there are suns in every galaxy. As many as the drops in each ocean or the strands of hair on every head.' There was an earnest quality to his tone, the yelp of a wondrous child who thinks he's being followed by the moon.

'Wow!' she egged him on, 'I've seen nothing past the seven seas. And even those I've only seen on Google Earth.'

'Yes', he added seriously, 'That's part of the problem of the human race... your galactic lack of exposure.'

'What are the other problems?' She zoomed into his bioluminescent hair, panning her camera towards the rear-view mirror. The lens caught a glimpse of his pupils - they were turning fluorescent orange. She caught him looking back, feeling him as a thought.

You think about race in ways that can divide you - the melanin in your skin, the language of your tongue, the limits of your motherlands. These do not make a race, all the other sentients in your galaxy remember that. Souls belonging to different galaxies make up its race. You are the soul of the Milky Way and the flesh of the Earth. The leopards, the rats, the viruses, each help their great mother except you. Your idea of a race has a finish line. The voices in her head often spoke with a dramatic flourish, but never had she consciously thought about her role in the Milky Way. There was never any time to think about those things. Her universe revolved around paying the bills. Surely, her mind was playing tricks. The rickshaw sped loudly towards the Bisleri factory. An uncanny silence swallowed the street. There was nothing in sight - no midnight *cyclewallas*[18] selling hot thermos coffee and cigarettes. No police patrol and *nakabandis*[19] hunting down trans-sexual prostitutes whose razzmatazz dresses turned the late-night street corner into a flashy disco. Everything was uncannily pristine, quiet, and empty. Wherever Afra's mysterious rickshaw drove, the streetlights fluctuated. By all accounts, it was shaping into a nearly impossible night. The moon played its part, bathing the streets with blue luminescence. Its full face shone with hypnotic force behind the glass façade of corporate buildings. Afra stared with unblinking eyes.

---

18 cyclists selling newspapers, tea, food items
19 a system of patrolling streets by using check-points

'If you're an alien, you should know… Is something up with the moon today? An eclipse? Strawberry full moon? Doesn't it seem really close?'

'Yes', he said, 'It may need to pull closer in… to bring the flood.'

'Is that what brings you here?' she asked the mysterious man. 'You're conspiring with the moon to flood us all?'

'No. That is the GN-z11 race's expertise', he said matter-of-factly. 'Us Shivenittikukas… We're the survey conductors of the cosmos. We only visit when the Milky Way calls. It wants a study to be conducted before the reset.'

Did a stranger share her unspoken dream, or was it simply a matter of coincidence? Had more people dreamt of a secret reset button than history could account for?

'So your race conducts surveys? The GN-whatever race does some other important stuff, and what does our race do?'

'Your race manages R&D for the cosmos', he answered. 'It's where thoughts come to experiment into new life forms.'

Afra chuckled. 'Whatever you may or may not be, I'll give you one thing. You are weird. Not sure if it's a good kind of weird, but at least it's refreshing… What is being researched and developed in my cosmos?'

Dreams, Afra felt transported again. *The Milky Way is the testing ground for the mind of the cosmos, it comes here to play. But you have moved far from the Earth's imaginations, and she is your host. She's not giving up on you entirely, like she did with dinosaurs, though you're tiring her out. Another flood will come to wipe most of you. Only the true ones will remain. The ones who still remember what it means to dream a good dream. The ones connected to the soul of the Milky Way.* Afra's mind-eye swirled with visions – of proteins duplicating into building blocks of life, of bacteria rising to the surface of the earth, of algae that stretched its arms into trees. Of carbon making tree barks from thin air, of shoots releasing oxygen into the skies. Of time and space germinating secrets into every seed, sperm and ovule. Of eyes that could marvel the work of stars. Of stars twinkling within each iris.

'Stop the ride.' Words felt light-years away; her head felt burdened as a planet.

'I will, once you've completed the survey.'

'What bloody survey?' Her head grew nebulous. 'Just stop the ride.'

The rear-view mirror no longer reflected any sort of pupils. Instead, his head projected outward in bright neon colours, lit like stars that swivel in a galaxy. The shed of the rickshaw transformed into a hologram. Afra and the rickshaw driver were connected by a swivel of cosmic dust. His voice echoed through her universe with deadly seriousness. *Do you dare to dream a good dream, Afra Sayeed? Do you dare to live like your dreams, Afra Sayeed?*

She hadn't let her name slip, nor was she wearing her employee badge for him to know. With a shoulder bag swung tightly on her tensed shoulder and a head bobbing in and out of a trance, Afra steadied herself to tumble out of the moving ride. She thrust herself out the side when the wheels came to a smooth halt. The rusted old building gate of her residence miraculously appeared right outside it. Afra scurried towards the safety of her housing compound.

'Watchman?' She banged the lock on the chain-bolt of the gate. 'Watchman?'

He snored cosily from inside his duty room, oblivious to the dangers of being a small speck in a strange, mysterious galaxy. Afra slipped her shoe out from her foot and banged it by the dusty iron gate rods, creating a commotion.

'Watchman! Watchman!'

A small, thin man slumped out of his cabin, grumbling along the way.

'Aaa raha hoon, aa raha hoon.' I'm coming. Lazily, he hunted for the key inside his pocket.

'Psst…' Afra whispered into the watchman's ears, paranoia glinting through her eyes. *'Woh hai kya? Mere peeche?'* Is he there? Behind me?

The watchman laughed. *'Iss se darr rahi hai kya? Toh humare cabin mein aa ke dekhiye, kitni chipkaliyan hai, sahib ko bol bol ke thak gaye, app bolenge kya unko?'* Is that scaring you? Imagine my plight, I sleep with lizards all around. Can you let the manager know? I'm tired of complaining.

Afra turned over her shoulder. A kitten crouched right behind, licking its paws unconcerned. The rickshaw was nowhere in sight. The bylanes leading to her home were lit with streetlights again. The alien and his ride had disappeared without a trace like a game of smoke and mirrors. She could not recollect when she walked up the three storeys of the building and reached her apartment door. Nor did she register her shaking hands while bolting herself into the safety of her home. A strange sort of exhaustion rattled her senses as she hit the couch. She fell into a deep sleep, a sleep whose intensity can only be experienced in moments when the body paralyses from terror.

In the dream, Afra was stranded at the Bisleri Factory crossroad during her midnight commute back from work. Her senses were rattled by engines of vehicles. The smell of burning fuel filled her chest, causing the usual pangs of anxiety. She daydreamed of total obliteration, and something about the night sky changed. An intimidating, grey soufflé of clouds made its way towards the busy traffic junction where they burst from their pregnant bellies with a thunderous roar. Down came a gush of pouring rain, so much rain, it lifted every wheel off the streets. The SUVs resembled bobbing boats floating in a stream of muddy, brown water, bathing every skin, mortar and brick in the gunk of the city. The gutters erupted from the earth's core, flying hundred feet upwards before they came crashing down spewing the shit of cockroaches, rats, and rodents. Afra's rickshaw bobbed in the surging tide until it capsized. Her limbs splashed in desperate rotation, reaching for the old streetlight's pole at the end of the road. She hugged the pole with all her might. A whirlpool sucked all that lay unanchored on the crossroad. The water morphed into shapes and forms of belligerent rage. It pattered, tattered, splashed with deafening violence. The skies roared with lashing rage as the water levels rose, and the streets turned into the rapids, pulling every man, woman, child, and tinned roof into its hungering pit. The sky roared thunderous and threateningly. A lightning bolt struck from the heavens down the spine of the highway, crushing it to half. Man and his man-made universe crumpled like ants under the foot of a giant.

A gem of hope flickered in shades of reds and blues. An unidentified flying object levitated through the angry skies. Neon tractor beams reached for a chosen few people who were saved from drowning as their bodies soared upward into the sky. Afra turned to the heavens with hope, calling out to the light beams above her.

'I'll dream a better dream', her croaky voice was subdued by gurgling currents. Her body pulled away from the lamp post. 'I'll dream a better dream.'

Her final words drowned in a giant Tsunami. Her mouth gushed for one last breath. Muddy, oily water burned down her wind-pipe. Her lungs collapsed with the force of a thousand pressing swords.

Afra jolted back to the waking world with a loud gasp. She sat in the passenger seat of a rickshaw; her head hit dangerously close to the steely meter.

'*Aye! Aaramat chalav naa.*' Ride carefully, she scolded.

'*Za na lavdya.*' Fuck off dickhead.

Yellow eyes gleamed one last time in the rear-view mirror before they were gone. The knob of the meter went back up; its screen flashed in fluorescent blue light: *Survey complete.*

7

HERO DE NOVO

Crows flew off the exposed ceiling of a crumbling, musty warehouse. A gunshot rattled rusted, old beams. The wounded heroine crouched on the floor between clouds of dust and debris. Her blow-dried hair and dewy, bronzed skin shone under a dramatic shaft of light. Her thick, full and bloodied lips parted in an exhausted sigh. Men the size and shape of giant gunny bags circled her with their lusty, menacing eyes. The heroine gritted her teeth at them and growled. With an athletic, aerial kick, she disarmed a beefy hitman and dislocated his jaw. A loud grunt and a thunderous war cry later, she flung an iron pipe at the mob. The front line of men fell like a pack of cards when another gang member raced towards her, slashing her mid-riff. She fell on her knees from the stinging pain. Crimson blood dripped on her fingers. The villains dragged her by the hair to their boss.

'Who's going to save you now?' the Big Baddie of the gang purred into her grimy hair, caressing her bloodied cheek with his bejewelled, sausage fingers.

The heroine spat blood. It spattered on his pristine, white *kurta*[20]. 'You should save your last words. *Shakaal*[21] is here.'

In the reflectors of the Big Baddie's cool blue sunglasses, a mythical shadow appeared. The drums surged to a crescendo. The screen lit the presence of a superstar who gave the pantheon of Indian Gods a run for their money. A hundred mythic arms shot out of his back like the limbs of a spider. His formidable frame smashed the warehouse floor, cracking the surface. He flung heavy-weight thugs across the warehouse walls as if they were empty cartons. Some men cracked their spines, others dislocated body parts as if they were loose screws falling off the walls. Shakaal axed, slayed, chopped, crushed, and minced the band of villains with the ease of swatting houseflies. None could withstand the force of an action hero with a hundred limbs. The Big Baddie of the gang was left with little choice but to descend into the lowest clichés of cowardice. With a knife to the wounded heroine's neck, he pressed the blade against her popping veins.

'Leave us, or I'll kill her.'

The superstar smirked. A charming dimple dented his left cheek. He swivelled his hundred hands; they moved with the intelligence of an octopus' tentacles or a *Natraj*[22] dance. His first and second hands swung out a cigar and lighter, his eighty-fifth arm pulled the Big Baddie by his pants, while his

---

20 a loose, long collarless shirt, usually worn with a salwar, churidars, or pyjama
21 time
22 the Hindu god Shiva, represented as a cosmic dancer

fifteenth arm snatched the knife out of the antagonist's grip and plunged it deep into his chest. The Big Baddie of the gang fell into a pool of blood. The wounded heroine fell into the myriad arms of her messiah.

The hundred-armed hero delivered his dialogue into the camera. 'When a girl says no, she means it. If only these pigs listened, they wouldn't have to die.'

As the lead stars of the movie shared a passionate kiss, a houseful of Bollywood enthusiasts clapped, cheered, and whistled with zealous fandom. Manzil Khan's performance as Shakaal sent electric waves across the cinema hall. Young girls stretched their hands, reaching for a touch of their movie God on the 3D screen. Respectable men and women jumped in their seats like a group of excitable chimpanzees. From the projection room behind the screen, Manzil Khan soaked in the moment. His hundred hands rested on his proud hips in perfect symmetry. The adulation was as sweet as tulips in springtime.

'They love you, Maz', Zubin took a celebratory swig of whiskey from the flask and passed it on.

'Tell me something I don't know', Manzil's handsome face wore an impish smile.

'Let's get you out before the show gets done… We don't want you bumping into the chimpanzees.' Zubin juggled his smartphones texting the entourage.

'I love chimpanzees. What's a star without a circus?'

'A wannabe.' Zubin answered with an earnestness Manzil had come to love about him.

'Have the paparazzi arrived?' Manzil flicked open a vintage skull-shaped compact mirror using his twenty-second wrist. His seventy-second hand ran a comb through his gelled hair. His ninety-second hand sprayed cologne.

'How do I look?' He flashed a pearly-white, dimpled smile.

'Like the envy of the world.' Zubin threw the backdoor gates wide open. The mythical superstar with a hundred hands waltzed out the fire exit, gracious as a dancing octopus. Out stood a dutiful army of shutterbugs. His hundred hands released like the petals of a lotus, putting on a show for the paparazzi. They threw themselves upon each other, fighting for the best shot. Manzil's bodyguards built a wall around him as he made his way to the car. He slid into the custom-made backseat of his Rolls Royce. Each of his hundred limbs fit into its own comfortable groove. He looked like a cosmic miracle, with limbs stretching out to make a perfect circle around his body and palms faced forward like an omnipresent deity blessing its many creations. Zubin sat in the front seat and instructed the chauffeur.

'Home, Balaram.'

On the highway billboards back from Wadala to Bandra, Manzil was greeted by his own stardom. His omnipresent, omnipotent, ambidextrous hands sold all that there was to sell - body sprays, chewing gums, polio drops, life insurance, science magazines, boxers, underwear and vests, political parties, and New Year parties. His rival and upcoming star, Lucky Singh, took the space on every alternating billboard - selling the exact same category of brands with only two hands and a more upmarket style. Manzil's top-left lip arched hatefully. Staring at his nemesis' air-brushed smiles through the window shield was never easy. He remembered the article he'd found on the way to the cinema:–'A DOORKNOB ACTS BETTER THAN MANZIL', the headline screamed. Below it was Lucky Singh's interview, citing Manzil and his brand of stardom as the reason the progression of Indian Cinema stalled. Manzil was cruelly labelled the *messiah of idiots* and a *performer without substance*. Every word of that interview hurt like a punch in the gut. Manzil couldn't get himself to read the whole article; his Adam's apple choked long before the last humiliating full-stop.

'He's a mockery, that Lucky.'

'C'mon now, love,' Zubin purred. 'We all know who's the real deal. Who's the star with a presence that shines like the rays of the sun?' He turned around with a jolly smile. Manzil inadvertently flexed his hundred biceps, which were cushioned comfortably in his throne at the back seat.

'I am,' Manzil whined. 'Which is why his face should be far from mine.'

Later that night, Manzil rested against the frame of his penthouse window. His shoulders bent inwards. Hundred hands knit into each other making a cocoon. He watched the tide of the Arabian Sea. It was a humid summer evening; the breeze still felt cold. Icy hands of melancholia gripped his heart. He could tell no one about this uneasy feeling. He didn't quite understand it himself. He was the outsider looking at the great mystery of life. The climb through the topsy-turvy ladder of cinema had left him dizzy. He'd ascended to a zenith no living human had found. Mumbai's city lights twinkled below his feet, the fear of falling clutched his heart. Zubin soundlessly appeared behind him, massaging his exhausted, lower back. His manager instinctively knew which part of Manzil's anatomy weighed down his stardom.

'You look unhappy,' Zubin whispered, kissing the back of his head.

'Because I am,' Manzil turned to meet his lover's concerned gaze. The plumage of hundred hands rotated with him, causing Zubin to duck when Manzil moved his shoulders. 'I don't know what I feel… Unfulfilled, maybe?'

'You're always jittery a day before the critics' review', Zubin offered helpfully. 'Superstars don't need validation. They just are!'

'Why do I care about these critics? I have a hundred bloody hands, and I'm still the one standing with a begging bowl. I have the masses on my side, and I still don't have one good review.' His restless hands got to work - the third hand sliced the olives, the ninety-seventh hand poured Gin and Vermouth. His ninth hand grabbed the ice-maker, his fifty-second hand shook the cocktail. The fingers on his hundredth hand sought out Zubin's. He poured the drinks, taking a long, bitter sip.

'People want me to be everything they want for themselves but can't have. They want to walk through fires, dive out of skies, fly into the oceans. They want to go beyond the limitations of money, food, and shelter. They want to dream with their eyes wide open. They want to leave their heads at home and be entertained. People want to forget that the world is a cruel, unfair place. But critics... critics can't see that about me, Zuby. They say my art is sexist, violent, repressive. They say my films aren't cinema... Why does my work break box-office records if I don't understand people? The world is escapist, and I'm a reflection of its wildest desires. Lucky's trying to steal that from me. He's been lobbying with the media to bring me down.' Manzil crushed his Martini glass with his bare hands, enjoying the sting of blood that oozed out of his injured palm. 'He's envious of my X-factor!'

'There, there, Maz. He's a fly on the wall.'

Zubin swooped in, taking him by the arm. They waltzed slowly; soft jazz filled the room with its pleasing tune.

Manzil's sedentary hands swirled slow as waves, opening and closing in a delicate dance.

'I'm going to make the biggest blockbuster this country has ever seen', he whispered to Zubin, who was cocooned in his arms. 'Success is the best revenge.'

'Best served cold', Zubin raised his small, bald head, extending his short, pudgy neck and reached for Manzil's lips. Manzil's high strung anxieties came to a fleeting rest. He closed his eyes and savoured the taste of his lover's lips. His hands ran down Zubin's backside when the phone buzzed relentlessly in the jeans' back-pocket. The world couldn't give a superstar one moment of real life to keep for himself.

Zubin sensed the distance and pulled away. 'What's the matter?'

'This is impossible', Manzil stared into the phone screen like he'd spotted his own ghost. Zubin nearly shrieked. The gadget in Manzil's hands flashed videos of Lucky Singh striking a pose that only Manzil could. A hundred hands soared out of his back, glorious as the rays of the sun. He was making a statement to the press - *Manzil's days of superstardom were done.*

A journalist raised her hand to ask him a giddy-eyed question. 'Manzil always maintained that he can do what a million hands can't. Now that you have the same hands, can you do more?'

Lucky pouted smugly into the camera—each mythic limb multi-tasked something personalised for the starry-eyed journalists in the crowd. One hand lifted a hundred-pound dumbbell, the other busied itself knitting an impressive jumper, some hands juggled colourful balls across his arms like rainbows, another wrapped roses into a bouquet and offered it to the said journalist.

'I've always maintained I could do with two hands what Manzil could do with a hundred. Now that I've found a way to level score... I could teach him a thing or two about acting as well.'

The room full of hungering journalists erupted with cheerful glee, enjoying his juicy bite. 'How did you manage to find his X-factor? Manzil is the only superstar in the world with a hundred hands.'

Lucky looked into the camera lens with a mysterious smile. 'I have my Guru...The great De Novo to thank.'

The audience of journalists pounced on Lucky with their zillion frenzied questions – *Who is De Novo? Where did Lucky find the guru? How can he prove to his fans that his new limbs are not just the work of some prosthetics? Would his limbs hold through scientific scrutiny like Manzil's did?* Lucky savoured the growing mystery of his superstardom, showering the audience with gifts conjured by the many tentacles rising out of his spine. Zubin switched off the television; the colour ran off his face.

'It's impossible, Maz. How did he? How could he?'

'De Novo.' Manzil dashed out of the lounge room, through the music room, across Zubin's library, into his personal screening room, past which lay a large thirty-footed wooden door that could only be accessed by a special code - *007*. His panicked fingers pressed the digits in a hurry. The door flew open to a sanctuary where none but Manzil went. A room with walls made of glass and water, filled with flora from around the world.

It was the sanctum of De Novo. Designed to please the aesthetics of the most discerning sentient on earth. Rocky slopes, coral conch shells, grey-black sands, mason jars, tropical waters, private islands and coastal crevices were custom designed for the cephalopod to spend his days discovering new corners in his endlessly imaginative sanctum. Manzil's hundred palms touched the glass, searching for the eyes of his nifty, old friend.

'De Novo?' he bent high and low, squinting his eyes to scan the smallest crevice.

'This is no time to play', Manzil walked up and down the glass surface of his hundred-foot aquarium. He searched for De Novo's polka-dotted red and blue body. Peering through coconut shells where the sentient often liked to sleep were empty.

'I'm worried, De Novo. I need to see you now, please?'

He'd sworn to save the mollusc from a world that didn't value small, gifted things. After all these years of keeping that promise, Manzil had failed.

When Manzil and De Novo first met, De Novo was caged in a small and smelly fish tank. Manzil himself had spent a few years living in shanties as mouldy as De Novo's home. Their connection was instantaneous - two souls recognising each other's worth in a world that wrote them off as inconsequential. Manzil cared for the life in the octopus' eyes. He cleaned the tank, fed him well, and enacted film dialogues for De Novo daily after work. The creature treated Manzil with a kind of dignity that human beings had lost for one another. The kindly mollusc opened portals of unimagined potential that changed Manzil's destiny forever.

'What is an X-factor? Where's mine?' Manzil riddled his wise friend at an unlicensed store, *"Happy Pets"*. Everyone was miserable in that pet-shop. Manzil worked there as a part-time salesman to make ends meet. The struggle to be noticed by casting agents wasn't a pretty one. Manzil needed money to look the part of a leading man. He'd been spotted thus far by none other than the searing eyes of a quiet octopus. In the reflective glass of the tank, Manzil looked into his own eyes. They were lacklustre. His hair was thinning.

'I've tried everything, De Novo. I've taken dance classes, horse riding classes, kung fu, jujitsu, karate classes, I've even taken a beauty and cooking course. What else do I need to change about myself? What is left to do?'

Manzil whispered into the fish tank. De Novo responded with a wriggle. He squirted out a dark, black ink, etching out an answer in calligraphic words. *Edit protein.*

'Of course, I take protein. Two scoops of whey, every day', Manzil answered naively. 'Six boiled eggs at breakfast… Boiled chicken breast for lunch and dinner.'

The eight-limbed invertebrate floated mystically, meeting Manzil's eyes where its dotted black iris unveiled a secret code. A code that took millions of years in the making. A cypher whose language was encrypted in the anatomy of every living thing on earth. De Novo often delivered deep truths in simple octopus ink. *'The protein in your RNA edits your DNA and your DNA edits you. Protein is the food of evolution. Protein makes the building blocks of the world. It can make anything you want. What do you want?'*

'I… I… I want to be a star', Manzil fumbled, overcome by dreams which had consumed him. 'I want to be a big, bright, shining star. A superstar.'

Tat Twam Asi, De Novo squirted out the words. A darker, bluish ink floated around, the calligraphy translated the Sanskrit script to English words. *That You Are.*

Manzil touched the glass of the fish tank meeting De Novo's extended tentacle. He was unsure if protein had miraculous properties that could make a superstar out of a commoner like him. But in De Novo, he trusted blindly. Hindi film dialogues taught him - *faith could move mountains.* De Novo spread his suckers wide across every arm, rotating in a cloud of thick, black ink that churned into a gamut of bioluminescent colours - flashing reds, oranges, greens, and violets until it turned a shade of gold. A liquid yellow colour emitted potent rays, bright as a star.

Drink Me, delicate words of sun-kissed ink appeared through the mist of clouds, dictating what Manzil had to do. *Drink Me.*

Manzil followed the eight-legged yogi's instructions. Bitter, thick, slimy liquid poured down his tongue, turning to vapours down the throat. Down in the pit of his belly, something clicked and spiralled upwards. His skin felt stretchy and rubbery. It expanded like dough. Muscle tissue tore from his back. The shirt ripped from the middle of the spine. A hundred limbs sprouted outwards, proud as the rays of the sun.

What followed thereafter, took the world's imagination by storm. A mythical superstar rose from among the masses as the messiah of their dreams, putting a sheen of fame, fortune and fandom on every film script he touched.

If it weren't for De Novo, Manzil would never have found the hundred hands that made history. If it weren't for De Novo, Manzil wouldn't be on the front of every magazine and newspaper, on the cover of every young girl's and boy's notebooks, on the poster of every newly launched product, on the panel discussions of conspiracy podcasts, or the centrepiece of scientific debates. He was the sun amidst the stars, the myth of the modern man, the freak show of destiny. No plastic surgeon in the world could've done what a simple mollusc with a large brain did for Manzil Khan.

Though not even the enlightened De Novo could be spared from the insolence of idiocy. The life of the polka-dotted sentient was in danger. Manzil wouldn't stop until he'd tasted the blood of the actor who dared to take him away. The phone buzzed. He picked the publicist's call.

'Find Lucky Singh for me. NOW!'

Manzil ran out of the empty sanctum, through the master bedroom, out the music room, past the lounge. He pulled on his custom-made leather jacket with a hundred armholes. His first hand grabbed the keys, his fiftieth hand pressed the elevator button, the rest of his four hundred and ninety fingers tapped the wall with restless frenzy.

'Be careful when you get there', Zubin said concerned. 'He's just as powerful as you now.'

Manzil kissed Zubin's forehead with the passion of a soldier bidding his lover adieu. 'No power comes between De Novo and me, not even another hundred hands.'

Before Zubin could say or do more, Manzil was inside the lift doors ready for the kill. His luxury sports coupe sped off Bandra-Worli Sea link, breaking police barricades and speed limits, whizzing past every sluggish car thronging the cable bridge. In the rear-view mirror, attention-seeking headlights flashed at him - the van of an entertainment journal was on his tail. The cameraman flung his head out the front seat just to get a good shot. A family of four crooned to the song from Manzil's latest film, and the children in the backseat squealed, spotting their favourite superstar in the car right beside them. They pulled down their windows hurriedly and screamed *Manziiiiil*. He sped off the growing commotion, breaking the red light. By the time Manzil's car tyres skid full-speed, screeching into Apollo Bunder Road, the imposing arches of the Gateway of India were cramped with a bandwagon of frenzied journalists, bloggers, curious fans and police cars, creating a jigsaw-like traffic jam on the tail of their favourite pied-piper.

Meanwhile, at the private dining room of a hotel overlooking the Gateway of India, Lucky Singh sat on a custom-made chair. His hundred new tentacles rested against the wall, making a beautiful peacock's throne for him to sit. He sipped a warm *shorba*[23] in meditative silence, staring at the seat across him with an expectant look.

'How's the soup, sir?' the chef popped in, eager to win praise.

'Like the nectar of the Gods', Lucky remarked dryly.

Across the stained-glass door, a shadow with multiple arms burst through the frame. The guest he'd waited for finally arrived.

'Give me back what's mine, and I'll forgive your filthy insecurities.' Manzil raised his chin, staring down at his nemesis. Lucky's multiple hands mirrored his own in every way - the work of proteins and the mollusc who knew how to build them up. Lucky slurped his soup aloud, savouring its flavour. He paused, yawned, and stretched all his spare limbs in a lazy gesture, opening his palms like synchronised blossoms. He continued eating his meal, looking rather bored. His blow-dried hair swayed annoyingly in the wind. Manzil's first hand lifted Lucky by his collar, the ninety-nine other palms closed into a tight fist, ready for a sucker punch. He spoke with rehearsed coldness.

'If you don't give De Novo back to me this very instant, I will crush your bones into dust, and turn that dust into the gluten-free bread I eat for breakfast.'

———————————

23 lentil and meat soup

Lucky and Manzil gave each other a look that suggested they weren't afraid of what was to come. Lucky wasn't going to back down without a fight. His ninety-eight hands mirrored the attack pose, and his first and last hands grabbed back at Manzil's collar. His mouth opened in an insulting burp. A tiny, wiggly morsel of seafood flew from Lucky's insides onto Manzil's cheek.

'That', Lucky sniggered coldly, 'is all that's left of De Novo.'

Manzil's fingers trembled. He stared at the tiny, semi-digested tentacle on his finger. His eye-rims filled with the tears of a broken promise. His breath grew uneven; rage tightened every muscle into a knot.

'Pity only you and I will know just what a genius that octopus truly was. I couldn't risk anyone else...' Before Lucky could utter another word out of his murderous mouth, Manzil head-butted him. The men flew straight through the glass door, tumbling into the private kitchen. Chefs scurried out as shards of glass shattered across the floor. Manzil pinned Lucky down by his chest. Unleashing the wrath of ninety-nine fists across Lucky's jaw until his molars flew out of his dislocated mouth.

'Why did you do it? You jealous bastard. Why did you do it?'

Lucky pushed his pelvic bone from under, toppling Manzil over. He grabbed a frying pan, hot off the burner, swinging it at Manzil's jaw. Manzil's seventy-seventh hand blocked the attack. Lucky responded with a barrage of fists. They collapsed in a frenzy of flying punches. Manzil tasted blood on his lips; it was a lot saltier and stingier than the corn syrup and food colouring which made the usual action prosthetic. No stunt-double was coming to his rescue. There'd be no retakes if he wouldn't avenge the death of De Novo.

His mind flashed with De Novo's helpless, kindly, polka-dotted limbs minced into tiny pieces, boiled into broth and consumed by Lucky's opportunist mouth. Guilt erupted like a volcano through his heart.

'Arrrrgh', Manzil jumped back on his feet. He grabbed cleavers, shears, hot pans, towels in defence. Lucky threw ceramic plates and bowls at him, fast as pellets in a gun. Manzil lunged at Lucky, slicing his left-hand limbs as they hit the floor. Lucky moaned in pain.

'Why did you do it?' Manzil bellowed into his face, choking him with a towel to the neck. Lucky dragged him backward, until both men summersaulted off the balcony and on to the street. A horde of their audiences flocked towards them. A manic cheer rippled through the fans; they grew roguish like typical football and cricket devotees. Manzil and Lucky groaned, their ribs cracked aloud. The audience around them cheered.

Manzil. Manzil. Clap. Clap. Clap.
Lucky. Lucky. Clap. Clap. Clap.

An intense, volcanic sense of destiny coursed through Manzil's body cells. The action hero would die a real-life hero. The villain would be minced to a thousand pieces. And De Novo would finally rest in peace. All his life, Manzil had chased glory. In death, he finally found a more worthy cause.

Manzil. Manzil. Clap. Clap. Clap.
Lucky. Lucky. Clap. Clap. Clap.

He slashed Lucky's twentieth and sixtieth arm and bellowed through his bleeding gums.

Lucky raised his tired head, smiling wickedly.

'Do you know what it's like to spend years sharpening your talent, paying for drama school, styling for portfolio shots, living with every rejected casting call, only to watch the least talented man get the job because he can pack theatres with his tricks? You remind me that substance doesn't sell, Manzil Khan. You remind me that people would rather be entertained than evoked. You're a reminder that the world loves gimmicks more than anything else. And that makes me mad. Really, really mad.'

He pierced a sharp meat knife through Manzil's back. Both men fell to the ground, bleeding by the litre. Their bodies were mangled and minced. The severed parts were awake, alert, and blessed by the de novo chromosomes of an octopus. All their fleshy muscles, digits, and bones slithered around one another. Divided limbs rose in rebellion, like the squiggling tentacles of a squid, or the tail of a lizard.

A stampede of people, a thousand-and-something in number, nudged each other for the best spots. Encircling their blood-soaked celebrities' fighter ring, they squealed with shock and awe as minced body parts duelled in an unparalleled street fight. The tarmac turned into a quivering mass of red sludge. The night grew darker. The air smelled of blood, slime, and bones. It was vengeful, violent, and vibrant. Fans stood around the remains of their favourite celebrities, chanting with an anthemic devotion that incited the spirit of a thousand parts and awakened the flesh of a hundred minced hands to chop each other down into infinite more pieces.

Manzil. Manzil. Clap. Clap. Clap.
Lucky. Lucky. Clap. Clap. Clap.

8

KIDNAPPINGS OF KOLIWADA

Wendy Patil's boat drifted seaward on the humid Mithi estuary. The mouth of the Arabian Sea glistened in ominous darkness. Stubborn rain clouds eclipsed the full moon. Ink-black, tidal waves splashed belligerently against the murky mangroves. Her oar pushed through the choppy sea, coughing lumps of plastic and silt with each stroke. A rabid and sickly river transitioned into a helpless and dying sea. Wendy could taste its suffocation in the winds. The tide had a queer way of pulling the world and its miseries into its belly, of accommodating the land and all its loonies. Marines grew saturated by the sins of a people who'd forgotten their debt to it, much in the same way they'd forgotten her *Baba*[24].

---

24 father

It had been three weeks since he went missing on those tributaries. Local authorities eagerly declared him sunken into the tide on account of going fishing on a rainy day. They just as eagerly cited his case to the *Koli*[25] community, signing off his fate as a tragic case of '*Look what happens if you go fishing on a rainy day*'. It was an insulting idea to say the least. Baba cited the monsoon as the time for the sea to rejuvenate its soul. He'd always say that a fisherman understood the sea, much like a gardener understood the earth, and a dreamer understood the stars. Baba hadn't come this deep into the mangroves on account of fetching the '*catch of the day*'. And Wendy wouldn't stop searching for him until she knew just what he'd come to find.

Vrukshpalli Ama Soyari. Nature is our friend. His raspy voice, sublime as the sound of the ocean in a conch shell, navigated her path with a compass' precision. Wendy pushed through the thicket of sooty shrubbery. Her oar dug through piles of plastic bags, greasy batteries, torn sanitary pads, soiled cardboard boxes, and the mangled clay bodies of Ganpati idols, following Baba's whisper. Her nostrils filled with the foul odour of decaying meat and excreta. *Vrukshpalli Ama Soyari.* His raucous echo came from somewhere closer to the seabed. There was no way to tell how deep the water was. Every jab at the floor unearthed more gutter.

'Baba?' She found it hard to breathe in that dense stench. Gasping from her mouth with her nose tightly pinched, she lay horizontally on the belly of the boat's wet floorboard. A current passed through the waters. Something moved through the slits between the wood. 'Baba?'

---

25 An indigenous community of people traditionally living along the coast of Mumbai, said to be one of the island's first inhabitants.

Her boat jerked with an abrupt, garish gesture. She toppled to its edge. Her head hit the stiff box of dry ice lying at the tail end of the vessel. A heinous creature revealed its face - the colour of grime with scales all over its skin. Its large and ivory fangs glistened in the dim of the night. Its coral, shell-shaped claws locked into the wood of the hull, twisting it around with intimidating strength. It hijacked the bow.

'Ghu'. It commanded in unpleasant high-pitched gibberish. Its slimy chest rose intimidatingly taller while it jolted the boat. 'Ghu-Ghu-Ghu.'

Fear clenched Wendy's throat. She lost control of her motor senses. Her mouth barely managed a whisper. The creature bobbed at the edges of her vessel, popping in and out of water. Filth splashed into the boat with its hostile sway. The longer she stayed immobilised, the surer she became of dying. Wendy grabbed her sickly bamboo oar with shaking hands. Swinging the paddle with all her strength, she smacked the creature between its scaly eyes. It shrieked loud as an injured puppy, falling back with a giant splash into the murky waters it had appeared from. Wendy neither stopped nor turned back until the boat reached the shore. Anchoring it into the safety of coastal sands, she sprinted into the world of in-landers. In the bustling alleyways, enthusiastic shoppers haggled for meats and vegetables like their lives depended on it, blissfully oblivious to the sea demons patrolling the creek right behind their kitchen windows.

'Where have you been?' *Ajji*, her paternal grandmother and eternal bore, sat on the floor mat right across the entrance door holding rosary prayer beads in her hand. She hadn't left sight of them since Baba had gone missing. Prayers had a strange effect on Ajji, the longer she chanted, the more aggrieved she became. Ajji stared at Wendy's worn-out chappals, dirty ankles and knees, demarcated with greasy blackness. She clenched her teeth, chipped from front and centre, growling in Koli.

'You foolish girl! What are you trying to do? Three more fishermen went missing last week. That monstrous sea has taken our whole life… What more do you want it to take from us?'

'What do you want me to do, you old idiot? Baba's body is still out there… Nobody's willing to find him. Do you want me to let your son die?' Though her heart was pounding louder than a horse, Wendy was no longer afraid of Ajji's bitter, old, cataract eyes. Grief had a funny way of mitigating her fears.

'He's already dead, you silly girl!' Ajji still wore Baba's old T-shirts. She had none of his patience or restraint. Her spectacles went foggy with rage. Her voice trembled. 'Why can't you pray for his soul with me? Why can't you stop causing him so much pain?'

Wendy snarled. 'If you want to call your noise a prayer, do it alone.'

Ajji erupted, standing on her wobbling feet, pointing her prayer beads at Wendy accusatorily. 'I pray so that Jesus watches over him. I pray so that your death wish out at sea doesn't come true. I pray so that you don't repeat his mistakes. I pray so that I can die in peace.'

Ajji's body was shaking with rage; she turned her face to the wall and tapped her forehead on its surface. 'This is all my fault. This is all my fault. I should have joined a missionary. I should've stayed a spinster. Only grief has come to my family. Only grief.'

Sometimes, Wendy wished the sea claimed Ajji in place of Baba. Without him, there was no adhesive to their relationship. They were always in discomfortingly close quarters of each other, seconds away from blowing each other's heads off.

'Matthew 5:4… Blessed are those who mourn for they will be comforted.' While Ajji went on murmuring verses to herself, Wendy climbed the small loft between the ceiling and the bathroom wall, curling on a tiny, cotton bed that was her private chamber. There was no point interrogating Ajji about demons at sea. Ajji was no less of a demon to Wendy. She was also the first person to introduce demons to Wendy's life.

'*If you waste your lunch, they will rise from the creek with their evil tongues to grab everything on the plate… And then, they'll eat you too. You little fool.*' Right from when she was a young girl, Ajji preferred coercion to conversation. '*The Lord expects that we gather all the last fragments of our leftovers so that nothing may ever be lost.*' Baba was the only one of the two adults who didn't treat Wendy like a lost island in need of rehabilitation.

'Are there really demons in the creek?' she asked with stubborn eyes, hoping to prove Ajji wrong.

'Anything we don't understand is a demon', Baba had tremendous depth in his voice, like the waves themselves were speaking. 'When you live in the spirit of the water and serve everything as a vessel of nature, you will see things exactly as they are. Neither good nor bad. Neither gods nor demons. Neither mine nor yours.'

'There's nothing in the sea then?' She needed to ensure she could throw away Ajji's awfully oily *teesriya*[26] the next day, without metaphysical consequences.

---

26 clams

'Oh, there's a lot there, Wendu', Baba looked towards the mouth of the grey sea, pensive.

'There's more mystery in these seas than there is in the stars. We must balance both these worlds… the one above and the one below.'

Baba's coarse hands expertly oared the boat, as if it were an extension of his arm. His playful brown eyes always saw through Wendy, as if she were an extension of his soul.

'Why must we do these boring things? Why can't we fish for demons!' Her little eyes were stubborn. She wouldn't stop until she demystified his riddles.

'What did I just tell you? Anything we don't understand is a demon.'

'I don't understand Ajji… Is she a demon?' Wendy's nose wrinkled as she did the math. Baba laughed aloud, his rounded belly pulsating.

'Yes, you can say that, but don't tell her I had anything to do with what you just said!'

Wendy pushed her little belly out, imitating her father's gregarious laugh. She wanted nothing more than to be just like him; time forbade her that wish. That night, Wendy tossed and turned in bed, wide awake, irate, and restless. Recollecting a tale Baba once told her - *the churning of the ocean of milk*. It was a curious tale, one that began as every myth did - with the struggle between gods and demons. The gods sought the elixir of immortality from the heart of the ocean's floor. They'd been weakened by the curse of a sage and urgently needed to re-instate their power. In an unlikely alliance, they invited demons to help them recover *amrita*, the elixir of immortality, from the depths of the cosmic ocean. To do so, the axis that balanced the world was torn out and used as a churning stick. It was steadied at the bottom of the ocean by an avatar of *Lord Vishnu*[27] - who appeared as a humble tortoise, holding the weight of the stick on his shell. While a demon, half-serpent and half-human, worked as a churning rope and pulled all kinds of wonderous things from the tide. In the churning of the ocean, many wonderful creations of nature came into being. *Chandra,* the moon, *Kamadhenu,* the cow of plenty, *Madira,* the goddess of wine, *Kalpavriksha,* the wish-fulfilling tree, various gems, celestial nymphs and finally, the supreme treasure, the *amrita.* As the elixir appeared from the ocean's floor, gods and demons broke their accord, battling one another for its possession.

Ghu, Baba whispered each time he began and ended the tale. *Ghu is the call of the ocean's floor. Where all things begin and end. Ghu.* Wendy sat up in bed, sensing Baba's presence. She felt certain he wanted her to meet the demons at the bottom of the ocean's floor. As Ajji's pressure-cooker-like snooze rhythms signalled her deep-trance sleep, Wendy climbed down the staircase and unlatched the creaky wooden door, making her way back towards the sludgy bank, ready to face her worst fears.

The air was exceptionally ripe with the scent of chemicals and fish bones. The sky looked atypically sullen and grey even for a monsoon morning. The tide was moody and unwelcoming. The sunlight was temperamental, hiding behind the mist. Wendy sank her toes into the grey, mossy bank. She pushed Baba's spare boat through the increasingly mucky soil. It bobbed supportively as it hit the sewage-laden

---

27 The concept of an avatar within Hinduism is most often associated with Vishnu, the preserver or sustainer aspect of God within the Hindu Pantheon. The avatars of Vishnu descend to empower the good and to destroy evil, thereby relieving the burden of the Earth.

current. She ferried her way deeper into the waters, a flapping sound trailed behind, suggesting she wasn't alone. She oared deeper into the water, feeling a familiar chill in her bones. A breezy haze pushed her into the axioms of the halophytes, which mushroomed dense as a fortress around her. She shoved through thorny, grubby plantations making her way back towards the Arabian Sea. Shards of plastic, cloth, clay, rubber and steel, rippled to the surface of water, in a circular motion. Her vessel tremored; camouflaged fins closed into their prey.

'Ghu-Ghu-Ghu.' Steady grunts rose to the surface. 'Ghu-Ghu-Ghu.'

The sea crumpled like wastepaper. The boat's floorboard cracked from its spine. Slimy liquid gushed through the cracks as the vessel capsized. Wendy choked to the vile taste of algae and kerosene. A hard-shelled claw grabbed her throat. Her legs and hands splashed around, trying to free herself away from its choking grip.

'Ghu-Ghu-Ghu
Ghu-Ghu-Ghu.'

The *Dariyalog*, the sea demons, fluttered their webbed feet, clapped their lobster-clawed hands, lashed their glassy tongues with devotion. The silt below their aquatic bodies reverberated with their war cries.

'Ghu-Ghu-Ghu
Ghu-Ghu-Ghu.'

Between them stood their leader - an archetypal creature, with acrylic scales, a coral-shaded body, webbed feet and hands flowing out of its limbs like royal tentacles. Its face was youthful and steely in equal measure, just as its gestures were both masculine and feminine. It raised its frilly, ribbon-fingers and the army of sea-monsters quietened down.

'Ghu. In the moons since the churn has begun, those who have entered our waters have not returned. With the noble efforts of all your gills, we shall churn the ocean of all its filth and take the elixir that is rightfully ours.'

The Dariyalog erupted with joy at the announcement of the timeline. They cheered in approval of their leader. 'Ghu-Ghu-Ghu.'

'Ghu. Time has come to take our cause across the seven seas. Swim for a thousand miles, swim till your gills hurt. Tell every sea demon to put their differences aside and prepare for the churning of the ocean floor. Tell them to spread their fins, tell them to unleash their fangs, tell them to release the spirit of the Ghu on every wicked creation of the gods. Instruct them to wreak havoc upon those who've forgotten their debts to the sea. Raise the tide until every boat, ship, and trawler crushes into our depths. Awaken every sleeping Kraken, recruit the swords of the Narwhals. Show no mercy to the wicked children of the gods. It's time to take what's rightfully ours. It's time to reclaim the sovereignty of our waters. Ghu.'

As the Dariyalog hollered in approval, Wendy came back to consciousness. Breath emitted out of her nostrils, as tiny as fish bubbles. Her hands, feet, and mouth were tied with sturdy ropes of sea-weed. To her left and right, captives like herself, stared into the face of their demonic abductors with disbelief. Chained by a string of seaweed, was a human chain waiting for execution - a marine guard, an old fisherwoman whose red draped saree drifted over her like an ominous river of blood, and a man wearing a tie that floated upwards like a noose. Wendy wondered if Baba was somewhere in this deep trench. She felt a tap on her shoulder; his reassuring echo rang through her eardrums. *Jyacha Maan Tyala,* acknowledge the function of each one.

His cryptic messages led her to a perilous end. Perhaps, the voices she'd been hearing were nothing more than his memories. Surely, Baba would not want her head snipped off by the claws of her monstrous abductors. The magnetic, coral leader of the Dariyalog sensed her growing uncertainty. He snuck up right beside her.

'Ghu. Tell me, god's evil creation... Do you want to live? Ghu?'

She trembled uncontrollably. Ivory fangs closed in. His gluey saliva touched her skin. His skull was thrice as big as hers.

'Ghu. Of course, you want to live. Everybody wants to live. So did we demons, but you did not let us live in peace. Ghu', the leader's glassy eyes turned cold. Its ribbon fingers icily lifted her chin. Her attention fell on the shadowy silhouettes floating above. A giant mass of creatures with webbed feet and hands loomed overhead, the way dead fish float on the surface of water. Their aquatic eyes were lifeless, their wavy hair was thinning and grey, their faces were colourless and sunken in. Tiny bubbles crept off their gills. Their scaly chests drew laboured breaths.

'Ghu. Do you know what's happening to them? Ghu.' His pointy teeth pressed against a vein on her neck, piercing slowly. 'Ghu. They're choking... From a slow, painful lack of oxygen in these waters. They're choking from the naïve trust us demons placed in your gods... I ask who of you is better than us? We, who live to preserve the sea, or you who live only to see it as a means to an end? The last time, we helped your gods find the elixir of life. This time, we will make no such mistake. Ghu.' Every rising word from his mouth was venomous. He bellowed at them all, every wail sent ripples through the dark waters. The leader of the Dariyalog smirked as it pulled back from breathing down Wendy's throat.

'Ghu. Our last generation was foolish enough to work with your kind. Now, where are your gods? They've all gone through the gates of heaven and left us in a world of hell… We should've known better than to trust them, but we're not our ancestors! We will hunt each one of you who returns to our waters. We will churn the ocean once again. We will overcome you and your gods. We will turn invincible. Ghu.'

He turned around to command his hungering army; his nose twitched with disdain. 'Ghu. I can't stand creatures that sweat from the skin. Kill them. Ghu.'

Before a sharp fang could rip her flesh and a fatal blow could snap her neck, an automated life-force took over. Though voice was hers, the tone was all Baba's.

'Ghu. You can churn the ocean all you want, but what if you can't balance it again? The last time you churned the ocean of milk, both demons and gods worked side by side, balancing the world's axis on the back of a tortoise and the spine of a snake. Yet, the poison in the ocean could've killed the strongest of gods and demons. Is it wise to try that experiment again in a world where the gods are absent and the demons are few?'

Wendy felt the stares of her own human counterparts resent her interruption. Her offence would cost them a slow, torturous end. Her voice trembled. 'Why ruin the one place you call home? What will you do if the ocean churns out of control?'

The waves around her froze. The water turned icy. The Dariyalog's animated eyes stared unblinkingly. Wendy grew quiet with an awkward close. 'Ghu.'

'Ghu. How dare this wicked creation of God speak to us this way! Does she think we demons have no powers? Let us show her how wrong she is. Ghu.' A slimy creature swam towards her with its fangs out like a shark.

'Ghu-Ghu-Ghu
Ghu-Ghu-Ghu.'

Wendy closed her eyes, ready to face the imminent end. A smaller voice amongst the ranks of the Dariyalog spoke in a meek voice.

'Ghu. Perhaps, the wicked creation of god isn't wrong. We should give her a chance to speak. Ghu.'

Once again, dissent broke through the ranks, the sea demons argued heatedly amongst themselves. The tides moved to the tune of their growing restlessness. Their leader broke their shrill chatter with one swish of its finger. Its hardened jaw tightened, it spoke with effeminate passion.

'Ghu. My fellow demons… do not make the mistake to trust the Gods or their wicked creations again. Ghu.'

'Ghu-Ghu-Ghu', the Dariyalog agreed to their great leader's justice. 'Ghu-Ghu-Ghu.'

Wendy summoned the last of her waning courage. 'What if there's no amrita left? What if there's no God at all? What if you all die in the pursuit of a myth that can't be found? I'm not asking you to save us. I'm asking you not to risk the only place you call home, just to destroy the world of god's wicked creations.'

The leader twisted its head; its cold eyes narrowed as she went on.

'You may not walk on the land, but you have the power to influence it. To save your world, wreck the land… And if that still doesn't work, go ahead and churn the ocean from deep within its core.' She bowed hurriedly. 'Ghu.'

Monstrous tentacles rose a hundred feet up against the Arabian Sea; the howling winds began motioning in a slow, backward churn. From the beaches of Chowpatti, the bureaucratic water closets at Rastrapati Bhawan, the fountains of every five-star hotel, and the gutters of every shanty, an unprecedented amount of gunk regurgitated outwards. Creeks coming from the oceans spilled onto the roads. Sewers clogged in backward currents until the highways were jammed with a tidal wave of gutter. Across the city line, people screamed from atop terraces with disbelief. Their alleys, freeways and crossroads turned into a giant dump. Most collapsed at the odour. Some choked under the weight of rubble. Back in the troughs under the sea, the Dariyalog broke the shackles of their prisoners free. Their waters turned a lighter shade of brown.

'Ghu. Tell every single evil creation of god the demons have returned for blood. Ghu.'

The sea monsters snipped loose the chains of their human captives. Every single life spared underwater would reach the land with tales of terror in their hearts. The myth of the demons would spread as far as the highest tree on the farthest mountain, and the clouds would carry the news across the atmosphere until every god knew just how lethal their adversaries were. As the other captives were escorted back ashore, Wendy was held back. The leader of the Dariyalog swam towards her with an oyster in hand.

'Ghu. We take no favours for free. Ghu.'

Wendy held the oyster in hand, knowing what she'd find inside it. Her eyes grew moist, even underwater.

'Did you kill him?' she asked in a small voice. The Dariyalog leader nodded unapologetically.

'Ghu. A straw pierced through our *Dariyaraja's*[28] gills and took our great leader's life. Your father promised to bring us the wicked creations of gods responsible for it. He failed to keep his promise in time. He knew what the spirit of the Ghu would do if he returned back to the sea. Ghu.'

'The sea ran in his veins', bubbles escaped her mouth, she choked. 'He was not a wicked creation of god.'

'You are all wicked creations of gods.' The stony-faced Dariyalog leader was unsympathetic to her loss. Before she could ask more questions about Baba's last moments, a webbed hand clasped her neck, and she went back into slumber. When she regained her senses, Wendy lay on a hill of shredded plastics and soiled waste. The ocean had spilled into the city like bleeding veins. The bylanes of Dharavi choked with peaks of grime and dirt. She looked at the empty estuary across her. It shimmered in pristine shades of blue, as clear as the sky. Wendy's silhouette stood on a mountain of muck and grime. The oyster thrust out of her dirty shorts' pocket. She opened its delicate shell. Inside, a large, white pearl steadily transmuted into stardust, waltzing like a wave of the ocean, as it made its way towards the sun.

'Thank you, Baba.' The pain of unknowing since the day he'd gone missing was finally relieved off her chest. She threw the oyster back into its rightful home, walking back into her ravaged new home.

---

28 king of the sea

Wendy hiked her way back deeper into the in-lands where rolling hills of industrial garbage, food, plastic, tin, and chemicals billowed over the roofs of tin huts and muddled alleyways. Smoke rose to the sky from the decomposing methane of the city's mounting topography of filth. Through the depths of the rubble, scavengers raised their opportunist heads, hunting for buried treasure that lay packed between layers of pungent odours. Crossing over a tattered pile of rubble, Wendy encountered a familiar face - the angry, gazing eyes of her grandmother trotting hurriedly over a hillock of grey and blue plastic. Despite the hundred-metre distance between them, Ajji commenced her lamentations and sermons with zealous energy and gritted teeth, the rosary beads in her hand swung angrily at Wendy.

'You fool! Where have you been? Look at what is happening here! Look at what has become of our streets!' Wendy walked towards her grandparent, disengaged. She was sympathetic to the cause of every demon. *Jyacha Maan Tyala,* she thought to herself bemused, acknowledge the function of each one.

9

THE LOST GODDESS

She was disguised as a hobo, standing on a busy interstate bus depot awaiting alms. Her outstretched hands were wrinkled, caked with dust. The heat was punishing. The atmosphere was deafening as the cackle of children after the last school bell. Vendors sold popcorn, sandwiches, and packaged water, with a charged whistle louder than the honk of eight-wheeled buses. Ticket-checkers waltzed through congested vans with the self-righteous air of kings. Weary travellers stomped one another's feet, rushing to find their luggage. In the sea of humanity, she stood all alone - a barren island clutching a begging bowl. She knew that about people: how little they sought miracles silently waiting to be found. She knew it just as she knew everything else: by being one and none of them.

She lit a *beedi*[29] between her dirty fingers, squatting at a dirty crossroad.

'Do you have another?' A boy stood across her, no older than nine. His floppy hair was streaked in shades of dust and grime. His front teeth were stained with betel-leaf juice, his eyes were bright as a rabbit's. She nodded her head, offering him a hit of nicotine. It wasn't appropriate for a boy his age to smoke, but the boy had lived more lives in his nine little years than most men lived in ninety. Of his life, she knew this - he was a nimble pickpocket and talented thief by day, who slept at an abandoned construction site by night. When he wasn't relieving sleepy travellers of their valuables, he was either scavenging for scraps from the depot's only canteen or dodging junkie-pedophiles who frequented the depot after dark to shoot smack. When he couldn't pocket things of worth, he survived on *chapatis*[30] stolen from puppies scavenging neighbourhood dustbins. Her spirit was pulled to the essence of others like a bee drawn to nectar. She knew it just as she knew everything else: by staring into every fractal of existence and seeing her own reflection.

'I can do a day without food, not without a smoke.' The boy smacked his crusty lips; his nails were dried with blood. 'What is your name?'

'You can call me M', she said. She was known by several names; one could go as far as to say she had the rare gift of being in many places at the same moment. But even all-powerful forms rusted, bent and slowed down with age on the earthly realm. The passing eons turned her into a deity who feared taking her own name.

---

29 a smoke made of cheap tobacco wrapped in dried leaves
30 Indian bread

'M?' The boy's face lit up with childish surprise. 'That's a cool name. My name is *Bhagwan*… I don't know which idiot named me that.'

'Why?' She received infinite information through every syllable he spoke. Phonetics struck her like chords of classical music; she could intoxicate herself with the history of a tone. In his tone, she caught the steely notes of bitterness.

'Look at me', the boy flicked his beedi into a gutter and tugged at a tuft of his hair. 'What kind of *Bhagwan*[31] begs on the street?'

'Oh, you'll be surprised', she smiled cryptically at the boy whose very name meant God. 'Look at any temple around you. Look at the size of their donation boxes. Bhagwans are out with their begging bowls all the time.'

'You're a funny woman', the boy chuckled while pulling out a packet of unopened cashew biscuits from under his oversized, torn shirt. She knew those biscuits were stolen from the tea-seller right across the signal, who'd been busy serving hot *chai*, tea, and *pakodas*, deep-fried vegetables, to a group of excited new arrivals in the city and hadn't noticed a little boy sneaking up behind his stall. She knew the boy would offer those biscuits to her in return for the smoke.

'Take one', he thrust the shiny, orange, foil-wrapped biscuits in her palms. Every act of kindness opened portals of transcendence for mortals to set one step closer to the heart of the cosmos. Unknowingly, the young boy made a selfless offering to the universe. She had no choice but to repay the debt.

'Won't you open the packet and eat one? Aren't you hungry?' the boy asked.

---

31 God

'No, my child', the Goddess said sadly. 'I stopped feeling hungry a long time ago.'

'Then why do you beg?'

'To redeem my soul from its eternal suffering.'

Her spirit was reduced to clay idols. Her omnipresence commercialised in temples capitalised by beady-eyed priests. Godmen made illustrious careers by declaring their desires as her divine will. She'd turned into a phenomenon bribed easier than common government officials. All this terrible fate had come to her by her doing - the game of dice she played with curses and boons. The weight of immortality and its many complications were cumbersome for a boy of nine. He squinted his face at her confusedly.

'I must repay your kindness', she said softly. 'I'd like to grant you a blessing.'

'A blessing? What's that?'

'It's like a dream coming true... What do you dream of?'

'I dream of not being hungry', he said matter-of-factly.

'You're a wise dreamer', the Goddess declared. 'There are two types of hunger you can dream away: the great hunger and the small hunger. The small hunger fills the belly and the pocket with everything money can buy. The great hunger fills the heart and the home with all things that aren't things at all. Which hunger would you like to fill?'

'I'm hungry for everything. Big and small things.' The boy was fidgety as children his age were meant to be, impatient to be gratified as all humans are. 'I want food, good food like *chowmein*[32]... I want more smokes. And a warm bath.'

'Wish granted', the Goddess whispered, running her hand through his hair.

------

32 stir-fried noodles

'Just like that?' the boy asked suspecting.

She nodded. The boy slipped his hand into the tattered shirt pocket. It grew lumpy on his chest. Out came a handful of chowmein. He stared at the twisty, red noodles bursting out of his pocket seams with disbelief.

'How did you do that? Are you some kind of a witch?'

'Forget who I am', she sighed. 'Run along now… And don't ask for more.'

The boy was reluctant to leave. With cheeks full of chowmein he stammered. 'B…bu..but how do I find you again? If I want to see you?'

'You will not want to find anything again, son. Every blessing is its own kind of curse.'

She turned around and walked away from the boy who would have followed her otherwise, save for the fact he no longer hungered for more than he had asked. As he made his way back into the semi-finished construction site that was his home, he'd find a floor in the building he'd never noticed before. On that floor, he'd find a grand, old tub glistening with warm and welcoming water and a fine, scented soap. He'd dip straight into the water and enjoy a refreshing bath. He'd think about who this mysterious beggar lady was and where she came from, he'd think of citing a small prayer in gratitude and realise he knew none. Then, when he was scrubbed clean and dry, he'd discover a loose *beedi* inside another one of his shirt pockets. The next day, he'd wake up to find he was no longer hungry: neither for food, nor water, not even for a walk in the sun. Every desire would be wiped out of his mind. Every thought would be free as a solar beam. In more ways than one, he'd be enlightened, at peace with the stillness and emptiness residing in the mystic heart of the universe. In that meditative calmness, the boy's mind would lose all connection with his body. He'd tap into a frequency existing only for beings nebulous and large as galaxies, transcending to a place where he was nothing more than a home for everything else. Ants would crawl up his nostrils and make a hill; dust would settle on his skin pores and find a home. The reeds and vines would curl through his hair until every part of him would be brimming with life like a bed of moss. He'd be rich and whole as the spirit of soil - a home where everything grows and lays to rest.

And she? She'd carry that unopened packet of cashew biscuits back to the tea-stall it was picked from, hoping to find more ways to redeem her soul.

She walked towards the rundown shanty balancing on four bamboo sticks where a tall, thin man in a *lungi*[33] prepared hot snacks and beverages for weary travellers stepping off the interstate buses. It was a crowded place; visitors chomped down handfuls of *vada-paos*[34] in big, hungry bites. She slid around the corners of the crowd, placing the unopened packet of biscuit back where it belonged. As soon as she turned to leave, she tripped on a traveller's luggage bag.

'Dekhke chal naa buddhi!' Watch it old hag! The weary traveller snarled. The man bore the look of a cruel master catching a servant red-handed. The Goddess was tempted to snip his self-righteous tongue out, but the balancing act of good and evil had evolved with more subtlety, even *karma* followed a civil code. She counted her breath till ten and watched the anger melt away. The tea-seller noticed her large, black, fiery eyes and stopped churning his pot of tea.

---

33 a garment for men similar to a sarong, wrapped around the waist and extending to the ankles
34 a fast-food dish of hot bread with potato patty

'Chch-chch', he whistled in her direction, like most Mumbaikars did when they didn't have the courtesy of time to know another person's name. '*Kai pahije?*' What do you want?

'*Kai Nahi.*' Nothing. She reached for the lice in her hair and chomped it down her throat, savouring the disgruntled look of the snappy traveller whose bag she had tripped on.

'Stand on the side', the tea-seller commanded in Marathi.

'I best be gone.'

'Stand on the side', the tea-seller repeated. 'I'll get you some tea once my orders are done.'

The Goddess had no choice left in the matter. Divinity demanded the divine's availability to return every selfless act of service. She stood on the sidewalk, watching travellers with watery eyes, swallowing fiery chillies that numbed their tongues and burned their bellies. Humans fetishized contradictions: experiencing all that the five senses offered while suffering at the hands of the very senses they craved for. The Goddess knew that just as she knew everything else: by living in the past, present and the future, all in the same moment. She resented the day she blessed apes with the intellect to use tools. And she resented the day she blessed men with the power of mysticism. Her devotees had turned into some of her worst mistakes, like the Khan Baba of Mumbra, whose misplaced compassion caused a racket of talking birds across her city. Something about the kindly eyes of the tea-seller reminded her of the old mystic of Mumbra. Something told her not to give away another grandiose blessing if she wasn't sure of where it would land on the panorama of space-time.

'Come and refresh yourself', the tea-seller brought her a fresh, sweet cup of tea that was his last.

'You're a kind man', she said wearily, sensing his kindness would sweep her off her feet. The Goddess had a track record of being swept away in the wrong direction. She sat with the tea without taking a sip.

'What's the matter?' the kindly tea-seller asked. 'Aren't you thirsty?'

'I must repay your kindness.' She felt the weight of the words deep in her chest.

'Don't repay me', the tea-seller wiped the sweat off his brow. 'Repay her. She's the mother who is kind. I'm just one of her children… A servant to mankind.'

He pointed to a small photo eclipsed behind a string of brightly packaged potato chips. She knew the picture - the coal skin, those penetrating eyes, and a tongue rolling red with rage. It was a portrait of the Goddess herself, as the mortals chose to remember her.

'Your eyes', the tea-seller smiled, offering her an empty bench to sit on. 'You have her eyes. It must be no coincidence, you and she share the same set of eyes.' '*Aai*,' he called her. Mother. 'You should pray to her.'

'I don't believe in the divinity of form', she despised the picture of an idol set in a shrine of her name. What could she tell mortals of a formless world, when language itself was such a constrictive form? A dialect invented for the purpose of mating calls, hunting and gossip fell short of interpreting the silence that lay beyond.

'I understand your cynicism. Aai will show you the way… She protects this land and its people. She protects all children who call her with love.'

Not even the gods were immune to the vanity of compliments. The more the Goddess fought back her blush, the more passionate the tea-seller grew in convincing her of her own greatness. He narrated his tale earnestly, with a type of simplicity that had long run out of fashion.

'I came here from a small village in Kerala with nothing in my pocket, save for a day's meal. I was only fifteen years old when I landed my first job. I painted movie posters on highway junctions. I rose through the ranks quickly, making more film posters than anyone of my peers. I worked on all the best films for twenty glorious years, until the printing business took every single one of us out of business. Out of desperation, I started selling tea. Can you imagine the fall? From working on blockbuster movie posters on the city's largest hoardings to reaching a time where no one knew my name, my work. When people forgot my craft, it's like they forgot me. I had a wife and three kids. I had a studio, cars, friends in the movie business. I had everything a man needs to live a good life. And then I had nothing... So, I know how you feel. I know what it means to be penniless, to wake up hungrier than you slept, to dream of nothing but living somebody else's life... But you don't know the power I found during that time.'

She knew what he was about to say, just as she knew everything else: by living in the spirit of all forms. He closed his tired eyes, feeling the strength of his belief course through his veins, whispering the words she knew he would speak. 'Faith... I found faith when I had nothing. And she gave me that faith... Aai.'

He pointed to her photograph again. 'There's an ancient tale about Mumbai... One that began when it was just an island of fishermen and Buddhist monks who lived on specks of land between the sea. During that time, there lived an evil force named Mubarak.'

She knew the legend: A demon named Mubarak terrorised the world with his enormous strength. Strength which led to arrogance, pride, and insatiable appetite for more power. Power made him want to own everything and everyone who crossed his path. Such power could only be destroyed by another being, with equal and opposite force. A being who possessed powers of the stars, the sun, and the soil. Someone who could be anyone and no one, someone who could destroy the mighty Mubarak with the force of a thousand Gods. And so the Goddess rose - an ordinary fisherwoman amongst the ranks of the mortals, blessed with celestial willpower, or so the myth went.

'So you see', the kindly-eyed tea-seller concluded proudly. 'When I heard that story, I realised in my time as a poster-painter, I found a brand of name and fame which made me proud and mighty. I spent no time with the family, though I had a wonderful home. I drank too much, complained all the time. I whored and gambled on the occasion. But I lived only for pleasure, and so I wasn't fulfilled. Aai willed my fall. She willed that I waken to the essence of what's true inside me. She killed my arrogance as she did for Mubarak.'

In truth, of course, the Goddess of Mumbai did not rise from the ranks of the people to defeat a demon. Gods and demons had been reduced to myths in the earthly realms because humans couldn't interpret a reality past the realm of symbols. The true reason was that every creator pined to be remembered by its creations, even if that meant it were a case of oversimplification, such as the caricature of a God.

'Pray to her', the tea-seller pushed the cup of sweet tea towards her. 'Pray to her so she may show you the way... And eat this food. It is my offering to the Goddess within you.'

The Goddess sat in stunned silence. She was drunk on the energy of his faith, consumed with the hope that this one blessing could redeem her city from its fate.

'There are two kinds of prayers', the Goddess whispered softly to the faithful devotee. 'One asks for the strength to take from the world what it dreams of, the other asks for the strength to give to the world what it can of itself. Do you know which prayer is real?'

The man stared at the sombre beggar in tattered robes with suspicious eyes. 'Who are you really?'

'Me?' A small, thin smile grew on her lips. 'I was born in the era of the Barren Billion, at a time when the Earth was just a hot, angry mess, full of poisonous gases. I waited in the womb of my angering mother until water vapour condensed under a thick toxic layer of gases and created clouds of acid rain. This was not an easy wait; it took millions of years for my mother's volcanic soul to lose her rage. That's when the magma made rocks, and rocks made lands. Lands that joined and split until they made masses large enough to hold the weight of continents, jungles, ravines, trenches, borders, nations, and cities of the future. I was born through the fissures and cracks of these lands, forged by a dance of friction under the earth's core. I have only one purpose: to create a world that can sustain more worlds within. Ecosystems and atmospheres for centuries of ideas. There are a million beings like me, born from the splits within the earth, but we have no form. Me and my people are known to you only as your Gods, but we are not like you at all, and we did not make you in our image. Because we are not people, we are the whole place. Every millisecond of history wrapped into one energy field. My strength is fiery as magma, my sight is panoramic as the winds, my heart is deep as the ocean. The elements made me, and I made the elements that came after. I made the waves lapping up on the shore and the grains of sand in the sea, the dirt of the hills and the clouds on the mountain peak. I made the bird singing on the tree and the snake that hunts it. I made the palm lines on your hands and the wrinkles on your forehead. I made the lover, the drunkard and the madman. I made the wife and the widow, the blood, bone and ash of everything. I am the Creator shaped by all that it makes. I'm a current that dwells within every place and person I ever made. I blessed all the wrong mortals and cursed far too many. And I've made a big, holy mess of everything I ever made.'

Her lips quivered like the last leaf hanging off an autumn tree. Her energy was sapped in the preservation of things she couldn't sustain. Her tresses, that once held the tide of the Arabian Sea in their flowy thicket, were now swarmed with angering sea demons, they prickled her being like an infestation of lice. The sky that was once clear as her eyes was clouded with the arrival of energies from distant galaxies intervening in matters of the Earth. Even her streets were no longer spared, she'd allowed too many myths to trample upon her land, too many Goddesses prowled her brothels, too many dreams bled across her alleys. Mumbai was drenched by the mistakes of the past. Its meaning had been lost in time. And its myths needed a new era of thinkers.

'You will redeem me', she whispered. 'You will redeem this place and make it whole again.'

The tea-seller got down on his knees; tears brimming down his unbelieving eyes. He saw the many faces of the energy field who he worshipped as a Goddess. Her skin grew slimy as a frog, scaly as a lizard, ghostly as a corpse. She laughed like a baby while howling like a lamb with a broken limb, in the same breath. He touched his head to her bare feet, overcome with devotion.

'Your destiny will alter a million moons, to you I grant the greatest of all my boons. You will re-write the history of time until all corners of space shall know your name. Every honour you ever had will return to you with the abundance of a thousand births. In return, I ask that you stay true to your prayer. Give the world what you can of yourself… Time has come to destroy that which cannot be preserved.'

The tea-seller held her coarse hand to his cheek and sobbed. 'Aai,' he repeated over and over. 'It is you. It is really you.' She wasn't just his mother; she was also the embers flying off his funeral pyre, but mortals didn't comprehend contradictions so large, and she didn't have the will to explain further. She knew the limitations of his predicament just as she knew everything else: by living in the synapses of an insect and the human brain. Yet, she would give this simpleton the boon of bending time, and by doing so, she would re-invent the present moment once again. The man would be transported like a slingshot in reverse motion, time-travelling back from Mumbai to *Bombay*, all the way to a place called *Bambai*. On that inhabited archipelago full of swamps and dangerous reeds, he'd land on the precise moment when *Agri* and *Koli* nomads looked out at the coast of Bassein and found the mast of sails they didn't recognise. As the first Portuguese ships docked at Bambai's murky sea, the tea-seller would stumble on the beach he wouldn't recognise, wondering which century he'd found himself in. The Portuguese invaders would capture the frightened time-traveller on their ship, while the kindly tea-seller tried explaining his derangement to them. He'd sob and laugh at the misery that befell no living man before him, wondering why the Goddess tested his soul in ways that he couldn't understand. Words would fail him; pantomimes wouldn't work. He'd have no totem of the world he came from, save for a tin box of tea wrapped between his lungi. And then, he'd understand the great game his Creator had played. The Portuguese invaders would spare the life of the time-travelling mad-man, most intrigued by the ordinary tin box of tea, because, in that time, tea drinking was indulgence yet to be found. The tea-seller would stumble and fumble, trying to explain how he was in possession of such a unique commodity. And he'd be paid a handsome amount to find just how to source more tea in the year 1534.

That momentary change in the thread of history, that destructive leap back into the past would send a ripple across space, untying the knots of every second that followed. The Goddess sat on the wooden bench at the busy interstate bus depot, watching the Mumbai of 2020 collapse on its head. The glass of the buses shattered. The buildings and bridges around the crossroad dissipated like granules of desert sand. People disappeared from around her like a wisp of smoke. Civilization vanished as it always had, with the ease of waking up from a dream. The Goddess smiled as she birthed a new world. Feeling at ease with the winds of change. Nothing was meant to last, and everything old would pass. As time and space bent to the energy field of Mumbai's creator, a new present moment was born -

A Mumbai that was lush and green, verdant with rolling hills and giant tea-gardens, dotted across the shimmering blue sea. Butterflies danced across the winds, sparrows chirped playful notes, elephants roamed between the forested pathways and crocodiles sunbathed between salty streams. The air smelled crisp and carbon-free. People were few and far in-between. The Goddess continued sitting on the bench that stood between the chasm of time, savouring the new *now* moment she had birthed from the boon to the tea-seller. This was the land she'd dreamed of: where trails were winding, long and filled with rivers without end. Gardens tinkered with the sounds of little bells along the way. Houses on hills were lit with the warmth of laughter rising from the belly. This was a Mumbai of beauty and wonder, a place more potent than the deepest dreams. There was no haze, nor dusty shanties, nor piles of garbage. Everything burst with vitality and life. Everyone was at ease to revel in the beauty of all that she had made. A group of brightly dressed tea-pluckers walked past her with bamboo baskets tied to their back, singing songs of rain and abundance. Their voices were sweet and soulful as the sea. The Goddess swayed to their melody, and the rustling tea leaves followed her lead in a slow swing. One of the labourers in the group noticed the wooden bench and the mysterious beggar who sat on it with a cup of tea in hand.

The Goddess noticed the temptation in the tea-plucker's eyes. She offered the cup which a kindly tea-seller had once left beside her. 'Would you like my tea?'

'Oh no, sister', the tea-labourer took pity on the Goddess' beggarly garb. 'You look like you need this tea more than me... Fuck Mumbai. This cursed city. Tea for the rich, nothing for the poor.'

The Goddess stirred in her seat, feeling her energy field stiffen as it did in the Mumbai of the old. The game of curses and boons had led her astray yet again. The world of forms had tricked formlessness. History was doomed to repeat itself as it always did.

'Isn't it cruel?' the labourer pat her face, gasping for air in the salty sea-breeze. 'They've planted acres of tea when there're millions of us without enough bread. Why not have more berries and trees that children can pluck fruits from, instead of growing leaves that only the rich can afford?'

The Goddess gulped, ready to digest the insult that was about to come her way.

'They say this city is protected by a Goddess', the labourer spat. 'I say that Goddess must be crazy to watch this madness go by and do nothing about it.'

Tea had turned into the most expensive commodity in Mumbai, and no kindly tea-sellers would redeem the Goddess of her latest mistake. She knew it just as she knew everything else: by living through the boons and the curses they brought.

If you have enjoyed the book, please take a few minutes and leave a review on Goodreads.com, Kindle or Apple store. Every review goes a long way in taking these stories closer to its true readership. Every reader goes a long way in enabling a writer. I cannot thank you enough for reaching here, for being the sort of reader who is curious to read these last words.

Do you want to drop in a query or just say hello? Write to me on snehsap@gmail.com

Acknowledgements

Mumbai - The city where I was born and my home of nearly thirty years. Mumbai shaped me in ways that decades in a city do - my identity, my expectations, my dreams are entwined within its history. A history born from a rare kind of audacity. A belief that anything is possible if you're willing to pay its price. Mumbai is that strange, toxic, hyper-cosmopolitan beast who summons the spirit of the restless, the desperate, and the audacious to do what it demands of them. Its tide is a temptress for all who cross its shores. Its horizon holds the next impossible quest. It is an ambition that neither sleeps nor rests. In the promise of its infinite opportunities lies the imminent chance of endless heartache, and those who dwell within its shores are eternally drunk on the possibility of finding the next big thing. I wrote these stories to encapsulate the ecstatic fantasy called the "City of Dreams" and imagined it as audaciously as the spirit of Mumbai taught me.

Birthing this book would not be possible without the support of friends and family, who've put up with the drama that simmers below every draft of writing, or the attempt to write decently. The creative path is long, lonesome and tricky. Some days, I've found myself at the peak on inspiration, while others I've struggled with thoughts that constrained my articulations. I've had the steady support of my long-time partner and boyfriend Rahul who has been my rock through this journey. I'm incredibly grateful to have a younger sister like Gayo, who has always backed me up when my nerves fail. I'd like to thank my editor Damian D'souza who accepted the ramblings of my first draft and turned it into a worthy read. And I don't know what I'd do without my mother who meticulously reads through every official word I write, because she knows I'm a terrible speller. I'd also like to acknowledge the kind-spirited critique of my earliest readers, Shreya, Chandani, Sharvari and Akshat, each of whom offered great insight for me to build these stories on. To my oldest friends, Sanchi, Insha, Paritosh, Diksha, Debbie, and Bajju who've generously lifted my spirits with bottles of wine and warm meals. And finally, in the months that I've carried this manuscript around with me, wondering how best to let it out into the world, I must thank the universe and its serendipity for connecting me with Valeriya Polyanchko - the cover designer of this book and a great uplifter of creative spirits. If it weren't for the sheer force of her brilliance, I'd have probably shelved this project and left my fate to the publishing business' roulette table.

The story 'Kamathipura' appeared in the Gaysi Family's biannual graphic zine in 2019. I hope the gender fluidity of these tales, make their own small contribution towards a world that looks past the differences of our anatomy in the times to come.

Author Note:

Sneh Sapru is an award-winning playwright of the critically acclaimed theatre shows 'Hello Farmaaish' and 'Elephant in the Room'. She's been nominated for the META Theatre Awards, the Hindu Playwright Award, and has won the Sultan Padamsee Award for 'Hello Farmaaish'. When she isn't cooking up new worlds, she dabbles at amateur doodling and stock trading. Weird people and weirder stories are at the heart of her biological chemistry. She lives with her boyfriend and their two dogs in India. Hens is her name spelt backward and her lateral better-half.

www.snehsapru.com